MW00573752

WEREBEAR SCARE

A Ruby True Magical Mystery 1

NOVA NELSON

FFS Media

Copyright © 2021 by Nova Nelson

All rights reserved. FFS Media and Nova Nelson reserve all rights to *Werebear Scare*. This work may not be shared or reproduced in any fashion without permission of the publisher and/or author. No part of this book may be reproduced in any form or by any electronic or mechanical means, including information storage and retrieval systems, without written permission from the author, except for the use of brief quotations in a book review.

Publisher's Note: This is a work of fiction. Names, characters, places, and incidents are a product of the author's imagination. Locales and public names are sometimes used for atmospheric purposes. Any resemblance to actual people, living or dead, or to businesses, companies, events, institutions, or locales is completely coincidental.

ISBN-13: 978-1-7367289-0-1

Cover Design © FFS Media LLC

Cover design by Molly Burton at cozycoverdesigns.com

Werebear Scare / Nova Nelson -- 2nd ed.

Previously published as *A Werebear Scare, True & Bloom 1*

www.eastwindwitches.com

CONTENTS

WEREBEAR SCARE

A Ruby True Magical Mystery 1

NOVA NELSON

FFS Media

Chapter One

Ruby True had never been a fan of leaving the house, even before she'd died the first time. But her Wednesday errands wouldn't run themselves.

So she finished putting away the now-clean griddle and dishes she'd used to cook a robust breakfast of eggs and sausages, and went to grab the proper outerwear from the hooks by her front door.

A chill ran down the psychic's spine. She'd long grown used to such a sensation, though, and turned to see two mostly transparent female spirits appear, hand in hand, through the wall that divided her parlor from the bathroom.

"Can I help you?" she asked.

"Huh?" said the taller of the two, looking around. "Oh dear!" she proclaimed once she took in the surroundings—the round oak table and chairs in the center of the open space, the small kitchen on the far side from her, the dozens of dusty totems hanging from the ceiling, and the middle-aged psychic medium with a shock of short red hair standing by the front door, preparing to run her mid-week errands.

"Pardon us," said the smaller spirit. "We weren't paying attention to our surroundings."

"And why would you?" asked Ruby pleasantly. "Well, if you're not in need of assistance, I humbly request you find somewhere else to hover. I'm just on my way out the door."

"Of course, of course. Sorry to bother you." And the ghosts floated back from where they'd appeared.

Ruby returned to her outerwear, slipping on a black loose-fitting knitted sweater over her black loose-fitting robes with ample pockets for all the necessary trinkets. There were a lot of things in her life she had no choice over, but comfortable clothing wasn't among them. So the choice in that matter was obvious.

Although Ruby had died once, unlike the two apparitions who had just stumbled into her home, she wasn't a ghost. No, that would be all too easy, and she'd never had that sort of luck.

Instead, when Ruby True's death came upon her at the tragic age of twenty-nine, she didn't linger on in the spirit realm or even die and go to Heaven (or the other place, though she was unsure it existed). Instead, she'd died and gone to Eastwind.

And it was in this strange little town where she was doomed or blessed—her attitude on it varied quite drastically from day to day—to spend the rest of her new life.

How long that would be, she wasn't sure. She'd been there for just over a decade and a half, and at forty-six, a woman of her age might expect a solid forty-six more years, barring any sort of grievous accident. But then again, there were people around town who were well into their hundreds... and some who were immortal.

So maybe age was just a number after all.

"Come, Clifford," she said, grabbing her black linen bag from its hook on the wall and pulling it over her shoulder.

From his place beside the fire rose a giant beast that, only moments before, the uninformed observer might have guessed to be a shaggy, red throw rug tossed over a stack of twin mattresses.

Clifford shook away the sleep and smacked his large jaws. Ruby noted, not for the first time, that the albino hellhound had taken quite naturally to domesticated life. (Of course, she'd never point that out to him.)

"What's on the docket today?" he asked through their silent connection.

After seventeen years, she was well used to speaking like this with her familiar. The communication had been effortless from the moment they'd first met, and her skill with it had only advanced with practice. For one, she'd become much more consistent with keeping him from hearing the thoughts that were meant for her mind and her mind alone.

"I need to return a few books to the library, pick up some tea and necromancy supplies from the Pixie Mixie, and then we're meeting a potential client."

Clifford trotted up to wait patiently by the door. *"Have we worked with this client before?"*

"Nope." Ruby opened the door for the hellhound, and he moved through just far enough for her to follow and shut it behind her. She didn't bother locking it;

3

anyone foolish enough to break into the home of a Fifth Wind usually got what he or she deserved before long.

And for those dark things that specifically sought out her kind, well, she'd already warded against them with a collection of magical talisman and charms dangling from her parlor ceiling. And while such things weren't directly effective against the living, the decor was usually successful at sending any other intruders packing. One time, eight years before, Goodman Fringer, a goblin who claimed he beat the largest ogre in Eastwind at a drinking contest, stumbled through Ruby's front door while she was sitting by the fire with a book in hand and Clifford at her feet. One hard look at a dangling mobile of bird skulls, and Goodman had run screaming from her home, slamming the door behind him.

And Ruby had gone straight back to her book.

She paused on her porch and breathed in the fresh air. It was a glorious spring day. She followed her familiar off the wooden porch of her little blue attached cottage and onto the cobblestone street, heading for the library at the center of town.

The town was alive with bustling folk of all types, as most every person in the small village seemed to have found an excuse to be outside. She could hardly blame them.

But it also meant she had to face more false smiles than usual. Because while the town's inhabitants were more than happy to benefit from her unique talents, that didn't mean they weren't deeply mistrustful of Fifth Wind witches. Whether that was because she was the only one of her kind in the entire realm and they lacked exposure or that her mere presence was a reminder of how close death was at any given moment, she wasn't sure. And it all came out to the same anyway, so what was the use of worrying about it?

"Ruby!" A voice like chalk skipping over sandpaper cut through the din of passersby.

She paused and turned toward the source. It wasn't hard to pick out who had called for her. The throngs parted for him as he approached, and she suspected it was done more out of fear than courtesy. Of course, there was really nothing to fear. This man was totally harmless.

Dressed in a long black cloak with a hood that covered his face, and gloves that obscured what she assumed were hands with no flesh or blood, the grim reaper waved and stopped just short of her.

"Good morning, Ted."

"Morning, Ruby. You look nice today."

Rather than asking if he was only saying that because her black attire was strikingly similar to his own, she smiled and said, "Thank you."

It wasn't that she loved wearing black every day, it was that—

Well, no, she did love wearing black every day. It made things simpler in her complicated life, and it also gave her an air of mystery that was quite effective in getting her clients to pay on time.

"Where you off to this morning?" Ted asked.

"Just some errands. And yourself? I assume you're not headed anywhere on official business."

Ted's official business was, well, *grim*.

"Nope. Not today. If everyone keeps living so well, I'm going to have to retire early! Heh."

She hated to think of what retirement for a reaper

meant. Did they play bocce ball with skulls? Perhaps knit funeral shrouds?

"Now you're just being judgmental," scolded Clifford.

"Stay out of my thoughts."

"Stop being so loud when you think."

She cleared her throat and refocused on the outward conversation at hand. "Thankfully you work in an industry with great job security. Especially in a melting pot of werewolves, witches, and dozens of other hostile populations." She paused. "Say, when was the last death in town?"

Ted had to think about it. "About a week ago, why?"

"Oh, I'm just meeting with a potential client. I don't know much about it, but her letter said something about it being a relatively new situation. If no one's died lately, then it's possible that it's not a haunting at all."

"Do people make false claims a lot?"

"Not intentionally."

He nodded, his dark hood billowing slightly but not enough to reveal the shadowed features of his face. "That makes sense. People are generally good."

"I'm impressed you're able to manage that level of optimism, seeing as how you're responsible for cleaning up every murdered person in the realm."

He shrugged, and the gesture created a sound like twigs snapping. "I've been around for millennia, and there are far more days where people aren't murdered than days when they are. At least around here. If you think about how often people *could* murder one another, well, it's quite amazing that I ever get down time. Heh."

Ruby arched her eyebrows. "That's an interesting

perspective, Ted. I'll have to think more on it. Thank you for sharing."

As soon as they parted ways, Clifford said, *"He couldn't be more wrong."*

"Agreed. But I do still admire his optimism, however misguided. I imagine it must take a great effort to keep those rose-colored glasses on his nose while everyone is trying to knock them off."

"I imagine it's a struggle to keep them on his face when he doesn't have a nose."

"Now, now, Cliff. That's just conjecture. For all we know, he could have a very pronounced nose underneath that hood."

"My coins are on straight skull."

Ruby sighed and patted her familiar's head. *"Yeah, I suppose mine are, too."*

The Eastwind Library didn't seem like a place Ruby would enjoy going, not because she didn't love books—she did, more than she loved most things—but because the mammoth structure was home to hundreds if not thousands of ghosts. Some people, it turned out, were too thirsty for knowledge to pass beyond the veil when their time came. And by some ancient and merciful enchantment, the library ghosts were able to lift the books from their shelves and turn the pages, a feat of physicality not usually within the wheelhouse of spirits.

However, the ghosts at the library didn't request Ruby's help like so many others did because they had no desire to move on, and none of the living cared much if they lingered. But that didn't mean that the spirits' existence within the confines of the place didn't unnerve most Eastwinders at least a little bit. With the exceptions of Ruby, Clifford, and only a handful of other beings in town, the ghosts were invisible. All anyone else saw was books levitating off the shelf and onto the nearby tables, and pages flipping of their own accord. And frequently one could glimpse the heavy floating tomes gut punching an unsuspecting living visitor as the deceased neglected to watch where they were going.

"Good morning, Helena," Ruby said, greeting the elf librarian. The woman would have been tall if she'd gotten up from her chair behind the desk, but she didn't bother. She held a book in her lap and only barely glanced up, not even moving her head in the act. "Morning, Ruby." She looked back down at the page.

"Okay then," Ruby said. "I'll just leave these right here for you." She pulled the books from the cloth bag on her shoulder and set them gently on the counter. *Sleep a Spell* had been a brilliantly informative book. But only once she was a few dozen pages into *Star Patterns for the Modern Age* had she discovered that it was a woefully outdated reference guide and might have stopped being relevant, oh, one hundred and fifty years ago. Out of curiosity, she'd looked for any signs or predictions in it of the last great war, way back at the founding of Eastwind, but discovered none. So it wasn't even accurate for its time.

The Were and the Maiden, however, was *quite* a good read, if a bit of a guilty pleasure. Although Ruby hadn't felt one ounce of guilt while reading it.

She cleared her throat. "You'll be sure to mark down that I've returned them?"

Without glancing up, Helena nodded.

Ruby pressed her lips together and managed to keep

her eye roll subtle. "Thank you," she said. It was always a smart idea to stay on the librarian's good side, and while Helena wasn't exactly friendly, Ruby knew this to be the elf's "good side."

Clifford trotted behind her down the stairs leading away from the library. *"You reckon they've restocked on those jerky treats at the Pixie Mixie?"*

She scratched him behind his ear, which was level with her shoulders. *"I'll ask."*

But as soon as they entered the Eastwind Emporium, the town's bustling farmer's market, Ruby's eyes fell on a complication.

There was always a complication, wasn't there?

But this one took on the form of a witch around Ruby's age grimacing and tugging at the collar of her dress as if it were choking her.

Except it wasn't the clothing that was cutting off her air, it was the hands of the ghost gripping the witch's windpipe.

"Time to earn a little goodwill in town, Cliff." She approached the witch. "Marjory! How are you doing today?"

The briefest flash of fear crossed the witch's face as her eyes landed on Ruby and Clifford cutting through the crowd toward her. "What do you want? I mean... How are you, Ruby?"

It was about what Ruby had expected from a Coven member, let alone a North Wind witch like Marjory. North Winds weren't especially social, something that Ruby was usually quick to forgive, viewing a disdain for chitchat as more of a virtue than a sin.

"I'm doing fine. How long as your neck been bothering you?"

Marjory's eyes grew wide. "Huh?"

Ruby repeated her question slowly.

"Oh, I don't know, three weeks?"

"If you'd like, I can help you out."

"How? Fifth Winds don't have healing powers."

Ruby chuckled. "There you're wrong. Close your eyes."

The North Wind seemed reluctant, but after scanning the crowd and presumably deciding that nothing too terrible would happen to her while surrounded by all these people, she did.

Ruby laid a gentle hand on Marjory's neck and then shot the ghost the sternest look she could. The spirit stuck out her tongue.

Okay, so she wouldn't relinquish her grasp of Marjory's neck willingly. That was fine. Ruby hadn't spent seventeen years refining her talents for nothing. She closed her eyes, breathed in deep, and recited silent words while conjuring the necessary images to complete the binding spell.

When she let her hand fall from Marjory, the North Wind opened her eyes, paused, blinked twice, then smiled with relief. "You... you did it!"

"Yes, I did." Ruby made an effort to keep from looking at the ghost, who was now spiritually shackled to her and cursing a blue streak.

Marjory thanked her profusely, but didn't attempt to offer any payment, which was about what Ruby had expected.

"Have a wonderful rest of your day."

Marjory nodded. "And if the pain comes back?"

"I should hope it doesn't. But if it does, come see me right away."

"If it does," Clifford said, "it means this woman can't stop herself from angering spirits to the point of them trying to strangle her."

"Indeed. And knowing what I do about Marjory's character, there's a strong chance she'll be a repeat customer. And next time won't be complimentary." She continued on her way to the apothecary.

"Here I was thinking you were just buying good will," added Clifford.

"You can buy multiple things at once... if you're willing to pay for it." She swatted gently at the angry spirit, who was now trying to strangle Ruby but doing little more than giving her a slight frog in her throat.

Ruby mumbled from the corner of her mouth, addressing the spirit, "You should know your anger is not unique. Every ghost like you I've ever met was nothing but a pain in the neck."

Thankfully, though, this one would be easy enough to manage as soon as she got the right ingredients from the next stop on her errands...

Chapter Two

The bell above the door chimed airily as Ruby and Clifford entered the dim space of Pixie Mixie Apothecary.

Kayleigh Lytefoot, one of the two pixies that ran the place, was helping a customer behind the front desk, but smiled and nodded at Ruby as she entered. "Be with you in a second."

"No need. I know my way around."

She usually confined herself to the main section where the herbs and teas were kept, and she *would* be visiting it before she left. But at the moment, she had more pressing matters wrapping their chilly fingers around her throat.

She made straight for the necromancy section to grab what she needed for a proper anchoring spell. She'd just run out of a few crucial ingredients the day before. She remembered the days when being out of butter or milk were what spurred her to finally go grocery shopping. Now it was any of the necessary ingredients she needed to pin a spirit to a single location so she could move about freely without the attachment.

Because the necromancy section was rarely frequented by patrons—and had contained little more than a few small jars beyond their expiration date before she'd come to town—it was situated in the far back corner of the apothecary. She weaved between two heavy wooden rows of shelves upon which glass bottles and small coffers filled the space and below which sat large barrels of bulk ingredients. Running through her shopping list in her head so as not to forget anything, she turned the corner and nearly ran straight into something, or rather someone, massive and rather solid. "Oh! Pardon me!"

She looked up and found herself staring into the stern face of a man—or, to be more precise, a werebear—whom she knew only casually. Despite it hardly being spring, his chocolate colored hair already had sun streaks of copper running through it, and his face, all clean corners and lines, looked like it might have been chiseled by one of the Italian masters.

Her mind jumped back to a steamy scene from *The Were and the Maiden* and she swallowed hard, trying to push the lurid images from her mind.

His stoic expression cracked and he grinned down at her through ocean-blue eyes. "Ruby True." His voice was deep and rich, and it washed over her.

"Zax Banderfield, if I'm not mistaken." She took a step back to allow herself a little space to breathe.

"I see my reputation precedes me."

"Of course it does," she said. "Everyone knows you sit on the High Council. And people talk."

There was a mischievous gleam in his eyes. "Are you intimidated, then?"

"As someone whose reputation also clearly precedes her, I could ask you the same."

"Me? Intimidated by you?" He leaned back and looked down at her small form, arching an eyebrow as he did.

"Oh please," she said, "size doesn't matter."

He grinned. "Sometimes it does."

Clifford stepped forward and growled, and Zax appeared taken aback. "Case in point," he said, motioning at the massive hellhound. "But to answer your question truthfully, yes, I'm a little intimidated."

"As you should be," she snipped. "No man, regardless of stature, is immune from a fear of death."

"Too true. But some learn to embrace it." He bowed his head politely. "Nice to officially meet you, Ruby. I hope we run into each other again soon." He paused. "But, you know, not in the course of your *professional* pursuits."

As another sultry scene from *The Were and the Maiden* spun its way through her mind, she refrained from commenting about mixing business with pleasure and instead said, "And nice to meet you as well."

He didn't depart right away, though. Instead, he added, "If you ever have occasion to visit Fluke Mountain, send me an owl ahead of time. I have connections at Treetop Lodge and most of the restaurants, and I'm happy to get you first-rate accommodations."

She offered him as platonic of a smile as she could muster. "Very kind of you, Zax. Now, if you'll excuse me, I have a ghost trying to literally strangle the life out of me at this very moment, and I'd like to attend to that."

She didn't miss the horror flash across his face before she and Clifford sidestepped him and made their way to the necromancy supplies.

As she shoveled what she needed into her a few small, burlap supply bags, tying the end of each in a knot before slipping it into her large woven tote, Kayleigh's voice caught her attention from a few aisles over. Clifford's floppy ears were already raised when Ruby froze to listen in.

"What kind of wounds, did you say?" Kayleigh asked.

The spirit squeezing Ruby's neck loosened her grip slightly and began yelling instead. Ruby shushed her quickly, not for fear of her being overheard, but so that Ruby could overhear the conversation a few rows away.

Sure, eavesdropping wasn't one of her nobler hobbies, but it had proven professionally useful more than not. Besides, something in her gut was telling her to listen up. And she'd be a fool to ignore her gut after all the times it had saved her hide.

Zax's baritone voice responded. "Gashes. From claws. Virgil didn't give me many details, only that he was in a bit of a scrape out in the Silent Reach on Monday."

"Is that common?" Kayleigh asked, sounding genuinely concerned.

"Not so much lately. Sometimes bears have it out— we prefer to settle disputes physically—but just between us,"—he lowered his voice, and Ruby instinctively leaned closer to the source—"these cuts were deep. The only times I've seen their match were on dead bears. He's lucky to be alive, especially after waiting a day to ask for help."

"Yes, he's lucky. Sounds like you'll need extra hidebehind fur to help pack the wounds," she said. "It's a little pricy, but it does wonders to prevent permanent scarring."

Ruby listened to Zax's heavy footsteps and the breezy flutter of Kayleigh's wings as the pixie led him away to the far side of the store.

Ruby glanced down at Clifford, neither saying a thing, even telepathically. It was obvious the hellhound was considering what he'd heard as well...

She didn't know much about Zax, other than the fact that he was head of the Eastwind werebear sleuth, sat on the High Council, and was as breathtaking to look at as an untouched mountain range at sunset. A part of her was secretly thrilled to know that he also took good care of his bears. Stopping by the Pixie Mixie for medical aid? She couldn't imagine a werewolf pack leader going to that effort, and forget about the High Priest doing that for one of his witches...

She discovered a newfound desire to visit Fluke Mountain sometime soon, despite never having thought twice about venturing that far outside the heart of town. It might be nice to move from cobblestone streets to piney foot trails. And maybe the spirits would have a more difficult time finding her if she weren't in her usual spot.

The ghostly hands tightened around her neck again, shocking her back to reality.

No, the spirits would still find her. They had a knack for it and nothing but time on their translucent hands.

Didn't matter. A vacation to Fluke Mountain was out for all kinds of reasons.

Ruby cleared her throat against the frog forming in it from the ongoing attempt to strangle her. While it helped clear her airway, it also prompted the ghost to try a new technique for causing Ruby pain, and she drove her fist into the Fifth Wind's stomach again and again, causing it to rumble audibly. That was a sign that it was time to get a move on if she ever knew one.

She gathered up the rest of the ingredients on her mental list and brought them up to the counter just as Zax was leaving with his goods. Kayleigh waved goodbye to him and sighed once he was out of sight. She blinked a few times as she turned to Ruby. "He's quite something, isn't he?"

Ruby hesitated. "Well, yes, I suppose, but I thought you weren't interested in..." She let the words hang, hoping the insinuation didn't offend.

Kayleigh chuckled breezily. "Just because I've chosen to spend my life with Stella doesn't mean I'm immune to the charms of someone like him."

"Fair enough," Ruby said, unloading the last of her baggies into the counter.

The pixie, who couldn't be more than three feet from head to toe, grabbed the first one, weighed it in her small hand as she fluttered steadily in midair, and added, "It's hard to imagine why a man like him would still be single."

Ruby sensed where this conversation was going and wasn't sure if she wanted to follow along. "Oh, it's not *that* hard."

Kayleigh's head shot up to look at her. "How do you mean?"

"Well, he's a bit full of himself, isn't he?" She thought of the look in his eye when he asked her if she found him intimidating. Ha! As if she would be intimidated just because he held power in this town and was tall enough that she could climb him like an evergreen tree...

Clifford growled from beside her. Had she let that thought seep through?

"Apologies," she said.

"What you think on your own time is your choice. Just leave me out of it."

Kayleigh shrugged and weighed another bag before jotting a line in her ledger. Then she asked, "Can a man be full of himself if he backs up all the hype?"

Ruby sighed. "That's a question for philosophers, and I'm afraid I don't qualify." Although, despite her lack of qualifications, it was a question she considered fully during her walk back to the house. And this time, she made sure Clifford didn't get a whiff of it.

Chapter Three

Stopping by her home before visiting the tearoom hadn't been in her initial plan for the morning, but neither had picking up an overly aggressive spirit attachment during her errands.

So, after unloading her haul from the Pixie Mixie and anchoring the spirit, Mirna, to a copper bowl on her parlor table, Ruby went to meet with her potential client.

If she had to leave her home, A New Leaf was where she preferred to be. Her love for a hot cuppa came second only to her love of being left alone to read a good book, and A New Leaf mirrored her appreciation for the drink. And because it was small and a handful of blocks away from Fulcrum Park at the center of town, the place had a calm and cozy feel to it that allowed her to breathe and savor the aromatic experience.

The client was already waiting for her when she and Clifford arrived. Clifford made straight for the large, overstuffed dog bed that the elderly owner, Harley Hardtimes, kept around specifically for the hellhound to lounge on while his witch conducted business or simply read and sipped her tea.

"Thanks for waiting," Ruby said, taking the seat opposite a frazzled faun woman. "I had a small business matter that came up."

The faun nodded, causing her tangle of dark curls to bounce almost comically around her face. On the whole, Ruby liked fauns. They had no long-standing grudges with any of the other creatures around town, unlike almost every other group. The worst tensions were undeniably between the witches and werewolves, the second worst between the leprechauns and pretty much everyone.

But this faun wasn't like most of the fauns Ruby had encountered. Sure, she had the same small horns, goat legs with hooves, and all the other *physical* features, but she also had dark circles under her eyes and seemed rattled to her core.

And Ruby's presence didn't seem immensely comforting. "Let's jump right to it, shall we, Mrs. Goldhorn? Tell me what you're experiencing."

The woman grabbed the cloth napkin from beside her empty teacup and began wringing it absentmindedly. "Things have gone missing. Small things, but lots of them. Sometimes they turn up in strange places, but mostly I haven't been able to find them anywhere." She went on describing a situation that, while puzzling, didn't strike Ruby as anything a typical ghost could or would do.

Once she'd run out of story to relate, Mrs. Goldhorn seemed much calmer. Or perhaps less jittery and more exhausted, which was about as much as Ruby could hope for.

"Yes, I see why you're concerned." Ruby placed her open hands on the tabletop, palms up, and said, "If you please."

Mrs. Goldhorn was hesitant but steadied herself and set her hands in Ruby's.

Ruby closed her eyes. Tapping into her Insight in a public place wasn't easy, but A New Leaf was familiar enough territory that it wasn't impossible. And she'd practiced this very skill many times before.

After a matter of a few short minutes, Ruby had seen in her mind's eye all that she'd needed to see.

She loosened her grip on the faun's hands. "Mrs. Goldhorn, do you by any chance have children?"

"Yes. William and I have twins."

"And are these twins, say, between the ages of eighteen months and three years?"

Mrs. Goldhorn blinked. "Yes. They'll be two years old next week."

"Right." Ruby sighed. "I didn't sense any traces of a spirit within your home. However, I did get a rather clear image of two toddlers slipping a series of small objects into their diapers." She paused and let the implication set into her formerly promising client. "I believe there might be a small cache of treasures hidden under one of your sofa cushions. But thankfully, your house is not, at present, haunted by anything beyond a couple of toddlers."

Mrs. Goldhorn forced a smile and nodded.

Ruby recognized that look. It was disappointment disguised at relief, and it appeared on the face of nearly every potential client to whom Ruby delivered this kind of news. Because as much as a haunting wasn't ideal, it *did* serve well to break up the monotony of everyday life, and some people were absolutely starving for a disruption to the mundane. She suspected most of them didn't even realize that about themselves until the moment when their ghostly concerns were laid to rest. Coming into the consultation, they likely believed themselves to be genuinely concerned about the possibility of a haunting and in a hurry to remove it... rather than excited that their humdrum life might be turned upside down.

After all, everyone wants to feel special or chosen in some way, even if the one doing the choosing is an entity hellbent on your destruction.

Once Mrs. Goldhorn had paid the small but fair consultation fee and left the tea shop, Harley approached with a hot cup of Ruby's favorite blend.

"Another dud?" he asked in his usual convivial tones. While most witches weren't so keen on Ruby and considered her a potential threat to their undisputed control in town, that had never been the case with Harley, even though he was an active Coven member and lived just down the street from the High Priest himself, out in the Copperstone Heights neighborhood. Harley spoke to her like a loving grandmother might. Not grandfather, no. There was nothing paternalistic about him, and she liked that more than she could say.

"Yes, I'm afraid so. But at least I made enough for the cost of the tea and, perhaps, a muffin?" She held up the two copper coins and Harley beamed.

"Looks like enough for a slice of the carrot cake, too, if you feel so inclined later."

"Oh, I suspect I'll feel so inclined."

He requested she give him a nod whenever she

needed more hot water, and she agreed. Although, the West Wind seemed to have a sixth sense for whenever she was ready for a refill.

She'd just taken the first cautious sip to test the temperature when the door of A New Leaf opened swiftly, and a tall, slender silhouette appeared in the doorway. A tall, slender silhouette with giant wings.

Sheriff Gabby Bloom spotted Ruby across the dim space of A New Leaf and smiled. She hadn't known the Fifth Wind would be here, but it wasn't a difficult guess. Bloom made straight for the psychic's table; there was business to discuss, and she couldn't afford to be away from the station for long.

Ruby motioned to the vacant chair across from her, and Bloom took it, looking to Harley Hardtimes and confirming with a nod that her usual would do.

Bloom angled her body in her seat so she could sling an arm over the back of her chair. "Fancy seeing you here."

Ruby was watching her intently with that usual twinkle in her eyes. Bloom had always thought that there was something about the Fifth Wind's air of confidence and curiosity that hinted the woman was only ever a few moments away from being neck-deep in serious danger... and wouldn't have it any other way (even if Ruby did constantly insist she'd rather be at home with a book). Maybe that was why Bloom enjoyed her company so much. Of course, as Sheriff of Eastwind, she couldn't openly admit that she enjoyed spending time with

troublemakers—or trouble magnets, as the case may be—
like Ruby True. Already, half the town thought she was
crazy for enlisting Ruby's help as often as she did,
regardless of the high success rate when the two
teamed up.

"Yes, fancy that," Ruby replied. "I know I'm
incredibly hard to find. I could be any of two places at
this time of day."

Bloom noticed a teacup-size half circle of moisture
on the table in front of her. "You just meet with a
client?"

Ruby sighed. "Potential client. Turns out her house is
literally crawling with kleptomaniacs in diapers. But no
ghosts."

Bloom was used to some of what Ruby said making
zero sense, so she let it go. "I might have some work for
you."

Ruby blew a raspberry, waving her off. "Oh, let's not
jump right into business before we've covered the
necessary pleasantries of gossip. You always have the best
of it."

Grinning, Bloom nodded. "You're right. I do." Harley
approached and she thanked him for her tea then waited
until he was out of earshot before diving into it. She
wasn't usually one for gossip, but it was refreshing to
listen to Ruby's take on it... because it was usually
Bloom's take on it, too. "I heard the Stringfellows threw
one heck of a second birthday party for their son last
weekend."

Ruby groaned, then looked around Harley, catching
his eye and nodding. She returned her attention to
Bloom. "You know I don't care about a couple of wealthy

East Winds and their mediocre toddler. Anything good on the High Council?"

"If there was anything juicy, you think I would know about it? They keep me as far away from their meetings as possible. The better to cut the entire sheriff's department budget." Bloom shrugged a shoulder and sipped her tea as Harley hurried over to refill Ruby's cup with more hot water.

"Okay, I've changed my mind," Ruby said once she'd thanked him and he'd left. "Your gossip is no good today. Tell me about what work you have for me." She wafted the fresh steam toward her nose, and in the process Bloom caught hints of jasmine and rose coming from it.

"The Manchesters say they heard something rumbling around their attic."

Ruby hardly looked up from her drink. "And they're sure it's not mice?"

"That's what they want someone else to find out." She watched Ruby for any signs of interest but found none.

"Could be that little son of theirs. He's quite rambunctious. Perhaps he's pulling a prank."

Bloom's eyebrows shot up incredulously. "Stuart? No way. He's the most straight-laced kid I've ever met. A little unsettling, actually... You know he scolded me for littering, back before he was even out of diapers?"

Now she had Ruby's interest. "You littered?"

"Of course not. I'd just tackled Kelsea Scandrick when she was fleeing Ezra's Magical Outfitters after robbing it, and a few of my feathers shook loose and floated past him and his mother on the street. That kid really handed it to me, I tell you. No, he wouldn't pull a prank on anyone. No sense of humor about him." She paused. "Do you want to check it out or not?"

"Do they know I have a consultation fee?"

Bloom groaned. "Ruby, *everyone* knows that by now. You're not exactly coy about it."

Ruby's posture straightened. "I think it's quite reasonable. I spend most of my days tending to false alarms. A lady has to eat."

"Of course a lady does. But we both know you're no lady." Bloom managed to keep a straight face until Ruby's rigid exterior cracked, then they both laughed.

The sheriff opened her mouth again, but she didn't get the words out before a clanging bell rang just inside the door. A message had arrived.

Harley hurried to the door and opened it, and an owl swooped in and landed on the table between Ruby and Bloom. It was careful not to knock over either of their drinks, and clutched the message in its claw. The small roll of owl parchment wasn't even secured, which meant someone had sent it in a hurry. But that was how most messages to the Eastwind Sheriff arrived.

Bloom pulled it open, her eyes scanning it closely, finishing it before immediately reading it again. Then she looked up at Ruby and, "Want to take a trip with me?"

"Where are we going?"

"Fluke Mountain."

Chapter Four

That she now found herself on the way to Fluke Mountain after thinking only an hour before that she wouldn't have occasion to visit was slightly serendipitous. Ruby wouldn't deny that. But she wasn't sure she would be of much use in this particular case, given what Bloom had relayed from the emergency message. But more importantly for her business, she definitely couldn't expect earning a consultation fee from it since she was accompanying Bloom on official police business and the sender of the message hadn't specifically requested Ruby's services.

"You know I'll only be useful if the missing person is not only dead, but has some unfinished business to attend to, right?" She tried not to sound so winded as they climbed the steep incline in the direction of Treetop Lodge. But when was the last time she'd exerted herself like this? Battling spirits was one thing, and while it definitely left her drained, it didn't usually leave her lungs in such a sorry condition as they were now. She wondered if she could grab ahold of Clifford's fur and have him help her along ...

Bloom didn't even seem to notice the extra exertion. "Yes, I realize that. But if this missing person went into the woods and was, say, murdered, don't you think he's likely to have some unfinished business?"

Ruby shrugged. "Perhaps. Depends on his self-awareness. Some people know they are at a high risk of being murdered based on the way they live their life and treat others. Those people generally accept their death as a natural byproduct of their poor choices and move on when that time comes."

"From what I've heard, Swamy Stormstruck is not that kind of person."

"Not self-aware?"

"No, not the type anyone would want to murder. I've certainly never had any dealings with him, and neither has Deputy Titterfield, to my knowledge. Oh, also, if you could *not* mention any of what you just said once we're around his concerned girlfriend, that would be extremely helpful."

"You wound me, Gabby. I have better sense than that."

Bloom didn't argue, but she also didn't agree. She merely grunted and kept walking.

They were just past the expansive wooden structure of Treetop Lodge when the address listed on the message came into view. Bloom led the way toward the modest home, and as they drew nearer, a hulking figure approached from down the small foot path that wove in front of the rows of residential cabins.

Zax Banderfield grinned as soon as his eyes fell on Ruby. He paused only a few feet ahead of them and nodded to the sheriff before turning his attention back to the Fifth Wind. "I had no idea you would take me up on the offer so soon."

"Don't get your fur up about it, Zax. I'm here on official business."

The sheriff looked back and forth between the pair, clearly trying to fill in the gaps; Ruby would catch her up on it later. She would also do her best to rid Bloom of whatever presumptions she was clearly forming about the two of them.

Zax sighed and addressed the sheriff. "Thanks for responding so quickly. I hope I'm not wasting your time. It's just that Opal was so distraught, she wouldn't relent until I sent word."

The four of them continued down the footpath, Bloom and Zax in front with Ruby and Clifford taking up the rear.

"And why didn't she send the owl herself?" Bloom asked the werebear.

"She thought you would respond quicker if someone on the High Council sent it."

Ruby suspected there might have been some truth to that, though Bloom would never admit such a thing. To say relations between the Sheriff's Department and the High Council were strained would be a tragic understatement. But the two needed each other, whether they ever admitted that or not, and Bloom was a practical person—she knew that her only hope of getting the budget to hire another deputy rested solely upon the whims of the High Council, and keeping them happy improved the odds that their whims would go her way.

However, as far as Ruby was aware, Bloom had no issues with Zax. At least she'd never mentioned him by name. But he was only one of seven, so his favor could only get anyone so far.

They reached the cabin's front porch, and Bloom planted herself on a mossy welcome mat and then turned to the others with a confident grin on her face. "Ready?" Ruby and Zax nodded, and the sheriff knocked on the door and announced herself.

A petit werebear with burgundy hair, and likely in her mid-twenties by the look of her, answered. Her bloodshot eyes and tear-stained shirt collar said what needed to be said, and when she stepped to the side, muffling a sob, Bloom led the way inside to the living room.

Zax sat next to Opal on a small love seat that faced two overstuffed wingback chairs. Ruby and Bloom made themselves comfortable in those.

"All clear," Clifford said after a quick sniff of the entryway and living room. His sense for immediate threats was the best Ruby had ever seen.

"Good boy. Have a seat."

Clifford didn't need to be told twice. He flopped down in front of the front door. Ruby knew that to be a strategic placement; his bulk kept any new variables to the social equation from bursting in unannounced.

Back on the love seat, Zax gave Opal's shoulder an awkward squeeze before breaking contact and keeping his hands to himself.

She may be one of his sleuth and under his

protection, but he knew boundaries. Ruby found that refreshing in a man.

"I understand you believe your boyfriend is missing?" Bloom said.

Opal stared down at her hands in her lap and nodded.

"And the two of you live together?"

Opal nodded again.

"Okay, so tell me what happened. When was the last time you saw him?"

For a moment, it didn't appear like she would reply, but then she sighed and shrugged at some thought she didn't bother sharing with the rest in the room and raised her chin slightly. However, she didn't meet the sheriff's eyes, instead opting to stare at the angel's leather boots. "He didn't come home last night."

Ruby sat silently, waiting for more information, but none was readily provided.

Bloom prodded, "And that's unusual?"

"Yes!" snapped Opal defensively, causing Ruby's eyes to shoot wide open. "He always comes home!"

"Forgive me," said the sheriff. "I'm probably not as knowledgeable about werebear customs as I should be."

Zax jumped in, smartly diffusing the situation. "It's not unusual for weres to go out on the prowl at night. The Silent Reach is designated werebear territory. Most everything else stays away from that part of Fluke Mountain, and because of that, there are almost never any issues with us shifting out there."

Ruby's mind leaped back to what she'd overheard him telling Kayleigh Lytefoot in the Pixie Mixie earlier. Perhaps that accounted for the "almost."

Bloom nodded and returned her attention to Opal. "Could he have gone out for a prowl and simply lost track of time out there? Or maybe he had to go straight to work?"

"No!" snapped Opal. "Swamy doesn't do that."

"A little defensive," said Ruby.

And Clifford replied, *"If she had hackles, they'd be raised."*

But while Ruby was losing patience with the woman's outbursts, Bloom remained cool as she collected the rest of the information. It felt to Ruby a little like getting blood from a stone (and not the cursed kind of stone that was reportedly found in the Deadwoods and bled profusely no matter what anyone did). But as long as she was able to keep her mouth shut and nothing was required of her, Ruby could school her facial expressions well enough.

She busied herself with a good look around the space. It was tidy, though there didn't seem to be any specific design theme with the decor. The two wingback chairs she and Bloom occupied were not only different shapes, but one was pink and the other yellow. And the loveseat was a boxy leather thing that would have looked more at home in a hunting lodge than a home. There were no pictures on the walls, but a few shelves carried dusty knickknacks that seemed more likely to be heirlooms than anything someone in her mid-twenties like Opal would have picked out.

Just as Ruby was thinking that this was the second dud of her day, Zax's deep voice interjected. "I know the policy is that a person isn't officially missing until they've been gone for forty-eight hours, but for what it's worth, I do feel like there's reason for concern in this case." He paused, his chest rising on a deep inhale before he continued.

"There have been, um, unusual rumblings lately. I can't exactly put my paw on it, but there's a malaise on the mountain. I know you're not in the business of investigating hunches, Sheriff, but my gut says Opal is right to worry. I know Swamy, and he's nothing if not responsible. He's not the type to stay out all night drinking or fooling around. And if he went straight from prowling to work, he would have sent word back to his woman." Opal nodded along, staring desperately at her sleuth leader like he was her only lifeline. "If it's not too much trouble"—he looked at Ruby now—"would you mind checking on the possibility that..." He didn't have to finish.

"I can reach out," she said. "But I'll need complete silence."

It wasn't true. She could do this with a little bit of noise, but if she could convince Opal to stop her whimpering, which seemed a little much for the situation at hand, all the better.

"Do you have a picture of him?" she asked before beginning. "I should know who I'm looking for."

Opal nodded and hurried out of the room and down the hall. She returned a moment later with a framed picture of her and Swamy eating roasted corn together underneath the Lunasa Festival archway.

That would do. Ruby studied the features of his face.

Then she shut her eyes.

After two decades of practice, Ruby was able to summon her astral nook immediately. The space looked different to each Fifth Wind, or at least that's what she'd read. Her astral nook appeared as a green stretch of soft grass along a lazy riverbank. The sky was always blue with cotton-ball clouds ornamenting it and the air was always that perfect temperature where one doesn't notice the temperature at all. The sun warmed her cheeks as she sat on a soft plaid blanket, sipped iced peach tea and watched the passersby. She'd been to the real version of this place only once before she'd died, but it'd left such an impression on her that when it came time to envision a meditative meeting place with the spirits, this one had immediately presented itself as the perfect venue. It was simply a canvas on which she practiced her art, but, boy, was it a nice one.

The path running parallel to the riverbank was crowded with souls enjoying their day. And good for them; considering they were all dead, they might as well enjoy it.

She scanned the faces gliding past, trying to spot Swamy. But after a few minutes of searching, she saw no blond men in their mid-twenties wandering by. Either he'd moved on beyond this spiritual waystation, or he wasn't dead.

She opened her eyes. "He's not there."

While that should have been a relief, it only caused Opal to emit a loud sob. She turned and pressed her face into Zax's thick arm, and he cringed slightly before patting her awkwardly on the back.

One of the things Ruby liked best about Sheriff Bloom was that when the angel was done, she was *done*. And it looked like they were almost to that point. Bloom smacked her hands on her knees, ready to stand, but Opal pulled her face away from Zax's arm and barked, "Wait! It could be something else. I didn't want to mention it if I didn't have to, but..."

Bloom narrowed her eyes on the young woman and delayed standing. "But?"

Zax shut his eyes like he was bracing for embarrassment, then mumbled, "If you're about to go where I think you are..." But Opal ignored him.

"Taurus," she said. "There's talk that Taurus has returned to the woods."

Ruby snuck a glance at the sheriff and was relieved to see the angel was as lost as she was.

Zax shook his head slowly. "It's not Taurus."

"Who's Taurus?" Bloom asked.

"No one," Zax said before Opal could jump in. "It's just a legend meant to scare cubs. It's not real."

"Tell that to Virgil Pine," Opal spat.

Ruby felt her ears perk up. Or maybe she was feeling that vicariously from Clifford. Virgil was a name she'd already heard today.

"Who is Virgil Pine?" Ruby asked, casually.

"Another werebear," said the sleuth leader firmly, as if that was the end of it.

"And something happened to him?" Ruby asked, feigning ignorance as best she could. It would do no good to admit to her earlier eavesdropping.

Opal nodded emphatically, almost victoriously, while Zax's eyes darted from Ruby to the sheriff. "He just got a little scratched up," he said.

Bloom nodded, as if that sufficed, though Ruby was sure the angel hadn't mentally glossed over the detail. As it was, though, Bloom's interest was already focused elsewhere. "And Taurus. Is he or she a werebear?"

"No," said Opal. "He's not. Taurus is a minotaur. And ancient one and the sworn enemy of werebears. He hunts us for sport."

Zax raised a flat hand between himself and Opal, as if cutting through the nonsense. "It's just a bunch of unicorn swirls, Sheriff. Like I said, Taurus is a legend."

Opal's face flushed a fresh shade of pink that had nothing to do with her crying. "So you think Virgil is lying about what he saw?"

Ruby didn't miss the tiny perturbed flare of Zax's nostrils. "Not at all. I think he *believes* he saw a minotaur attacking him. But as someone who's been attacked his fair share of times, I can tell you that it's extremely difficult to make sense of what is happening when you're in the moment and claws and fur are flashing."

"Is it possible," Ruby said, "that it *was* a minotaur who attacked Virgil?"

Zax grimaced. "I suppose, but it would be highly unlikely. The few who live in Eastwind don't come up on Fluke Mountain, let alone to the Silent Reach. They know it's werebear territory, and they don't want to start anything. From what I've heard, they prefer the Deadwoods."

"That's what I've heard as well," Bloom confirmed. "But we can certainly speak with a few of them and see if they know of any of their kind straying this way. And we'll definitely have a word with Virgil."

Though it wasn't an outright acceptance of the Taurus theory, that plan worked to temporarily subdue Opal's emotions. And after Bloom promised to give

Swamy's disappearance top priority, Opal allowed them to leave without a fuss.

But Ruby knew the workday was far from over. Her Insight was practically screaming at her: *Virgil! Virgil! Virgil!*

Chapter Five

Opal closed the door behind them, remaining inside and allowing Zax a minute alone with Ruby and Bloom. The sheriff could tell there was something more he wanted to say to them. She sensed it almost as strongly as she'd sensed the strange, nebulous guilt issuing from Opal in heavy waves just moments before.

As soon as they were a safe distance from the home, Zax confirmed Bloom's suspicion, saying, "Please don't listen to anything about Taurus."

"Don't worry," said Bloom. "We aren't. But the fact that the rumor has been floating around and now there's been one attack and one disappearance, well, I don't think it's entirely insignificant." She paused, narrowing her eyes at him. "Where do you think Swamy is?"

"No clue. He's a quiet man. The kind to sit back and observe more than participate. Opal is a bit much to handle, if you couldn't tell, and they balance each other out, I've always thought. But Swamy never struck me as a simple man. You can tell there's a lot going on behind those eyes. But he never causes any trouble, so I've never had reason to suspect anything churning in that brain of his is anything but good." He shrugged, throwing his arms into the air defeatedly. "Although who even knows? Maybe he *is* a little slow on the uptake and all that thinking is necessary for him to walk and breathe at the same time."

Bloom asked, "Is it possible he went into the Deadwoods?"

"Anything's possible. I warn all my bears away from it, but some prefer the danger of it. As far as I'm aware, Swamy was never one of those."

The sheriff nodded. "Well, let us know if you hear anything from him. If we still haven't located him by tomorrow, we'll set up an official search party. Deputy Titterfield can lead it. One last thing—where could I find Virgil Pine?"

Zax considered it. "Probably at work. He waits tables at Treetop Lodge. He should be there."

Bloom thanked him, and he nodded before addressing Ruby. "I hope your visit to Fluke Mountain was everything you thought it'd be."

She grinned. "Oh yes."

"Enough to bring you back?"

"Let's hope not. Not under these circumstances, at least."

He chuckled. "Certainly not." Then he reached in his pocket and pulled out a silver coin. "But just in case, here's a little something for the trouble of keeping your Fifth Wind eye open for any sign of Swamy."

Ruby hesitated only a moment before taking the coin from him and slipping it into her pocket. "Fair enough."

Typical, thought Bloom. Then, *But good for her*.

As the women and Clifford approached the front of the lodge, having parted ways with the werebear, Bloom could hold it in no longer. "I wouldn't have guessed him as your type," she said.

"And you would have been right," Ruby replied quickly.

Good goddess, why wouldn't the witch just admit it? It might do her a little good to find a nice gentleman suitor and have a little romp. And if that gentleman suitor was also a member of the High Council, well, that favorable connection wouldn't ruin Bloom's day. Obviously, Ruby's happiness came first, but if there was a side benefit for the Sheriff's Department in it, it was Bloom's duty to embrace that. Her civic duty, no less. "Deny it all you want, but I saw the way you two looked at each other."

"I have no idea what you mean."

"You can't deny he's easy on the eyes."

"I won't even try denying that. Now, back to business, what was your read on Opal?"

The sheriff shrugged and decided to give it a rest... for now. "About what you would guess. Guilt pulsing from her. I doubt you need my special powers of judgement to have sensed that, though."

"Guilty as in she has something to do with his disappearance?"

"Possibly. All I could tell was that the guilt had to do with their relationship, but you know how messy romantic relationships can get."

"I don't, actually."

Bloom stopped walking, and Ruby did the same, looking up into the angel's soft face.

"Ezra?" Bloom said.

Ruby rolled her eyes. "That wasn't even a little bit complicated. It was quite simple, actually. That's why I had no problem breaking it off."

Unbelievable, thought Bloom, remembering how long that particular break-up had dragged out. That was one of the benefits of being immortal—a memory like a steel trap. Not only did it benefit her in the line of duty, but it meant she could keep track of history in a much more accurate way than most mortals. And Ruby's relationship with Ezra, especially the end of it, had been anything but simple.

"Do you consider every matter simple?" the angel asked.

Ruby appeared undeterred. "Perhaps I just see no reason to make things complicated."

Bloom sighed, but relented. For now. "And perhaps that's why I like you."

* * *

The lobby of Treetop Lodge smelled like evergreen and earth, not too unlike the outdoors they'd just left, but with a hint of something sweeter and cleaner in the mix. Lemon, perhaps? People whom Ruby presumed to be werebears lounged around on the oversized leather couches near a twenty-foot fireplace, reading, talking softly, or simply napping. Ruby hadn't spent much time around werebears, but she suspected, based on the current observed behavior, she might get on with them quite well on the whole.

Virgil worked in the restaurant of the lodge, and a kind woman at the front desk directed them toward it, but not before eyeing Bloom's badge with poorly disguised concern.

The fact that everyone acted that way whenever Gabby Bloom went anywhere was one of Ruby's favorite parts about teaming up with the angel. She quite enjoyed discovering how each new person reacted to the sheriff's presence. Some of the facial tics she'd observed while folks struggled to hide their mingling reverence and contempt could be quite entertaining. One time, years ago, she and Bloom had arrived at the home of a murderous werewolf, and the simple sight of the sheriff had set the suspect to drooling uncontrollably.

Although, it was rare anyone was so obvious with their emotions. So, Ruby had developed a hobby of close inspection.

No one at Treetop Lodge had even gotten close to drooling. They seemed to exhibit the usual amount of paranoia at seeing law enforcement (*and* a Fifth Wind—always unnerving) show up unexpectedly.

Ruby, Bloom, and Clifford stopped at the host stand and, as they waited to be greeted, Ruby looked around. Early supper diners occupied a few of the tables, but business still appeared rather slow. However, the earthy scents of the lobby were now overpowered by the strong, savory smell of beef stew. Her mouth watered. If anyone knew how to prepare meat, it would be the werebears. The werewolves didn't strike her as the type to have the patience or the desire to put that much effort into their food. When it came to raw meat, though, they did hold a strong appreciation, and for that reason they had a bit of a lock on the butcher scene around town.

"Maybe we should forget this whole investigation and grab something to eat," Sheriff Bloom murmured, practically reading Ruby's mind.

"I don't see why we couldn't do both."

"*I'm in,*" came Clifford's deep voice.

But before a host came by and tempted them with an offer of a table, Bloom nodded at a waiter across the dining room and said, "That must be him. He looks like every Pine I've ever met."

Ruby hadn't met a Pine before, so she couldn't vouch for that. But she did take in the young man's appearance carefully, for future reference. He looked to be in his early twenties and was broad shouldered, likely a few inches shorter than Bloom, although that didn't mean he was short. His skin was chestnut brown from the sun, and his face was a bit bland, but not unpleasing.

She was grateful to have seen him first in a candid moment, when he was lost in his duties and didn't know he was being observed, likely so deep in his own routines that he wasn't consciously doing anything. Those were the most telling moments, in her opinion. You could glean a lot from a person's expression when it was at its baseline. And his expression was one of moderate consternation—his eyes pinched slightly at the outer edges, his lips parted gently with the corners turned down in a mild grimace like the world itself was just a little too much for him to make sense of.

"More importantly," Ruby added, "look at his arm."

His forearm was wrapped in a cloth bandage as he

carried out a steamy tray and placed each plate in front of the couple at the table.

"Defensive wounds if I ever saw them," Bloom said before she strode forward, heading not directly for him but back toward the kitchen to cut him off.

"Virgil Pine?" she said when he approached cautiously.

He blinked rapidly, jolting out of the flow of his routine. "Yes, ma'am, Sheriff. What can I do for you?" His attention jumped to Ruby, who grinned at him but said nothing.

"We were just chatting with Zax Banderfield, and he said we ought to come ask you about what happened in the woods the other night."

His parted lips pressed tightly together, and he froze momentarily before looking around. "Let me put this tray away and I'll meet you out back."

Ruby and Bloom agreed, and after waiting for close to five minutes, Ruby was growing anxious. But no sooner had she asked Bloom, "You think he took off?" before the back door swung open and Virgil stepped out.

He appeared slightly less agitated than before when he said, "Sorry, had to get someone to cover my tables. What can I help you with?"

Sheriff Bloom took the lead. "Just the story of what happened to you. I understand you got in a tussle with a werebear?"

"It wasn't a werebear," he said sharply, but the frightened expression that followed his words indicated that he wished he could take them back.

Bloom nodded sympathetically. "What was it then?"

His gaze jumped between the two women. "It was a... well, I don't really know."

Feeling her stomach grumble and remembering the delicious scent of stew, Ruby was about ready to move on with her day, preferably landing somewhere that served warm meats (Clifford would back her up on that decision, she was sure), and she wanted to get to the point. "We heard you believe Taurus attacked you."

Virgil, who may not have been exceptionally tall but made up for it in muscle, blinked nervously. "Zax told you that?"

"Yes," Ruby said. "Did you lie to him? Was it not Taurus?"

He inhaled deeply, puffing up his chest, then deflated and said, "No, it was Taurus. I'd swear it on my life."

Bloom cut in, "Now, from my understanding of the situation and the legend of Taurus, there *is* a slight possibility that you were simply attacked by a local minotaur rather than the one from the stories, correct?"

"No," Virgil said stubbornly. "It wasn't a minotaur."

Bloom was undeterred. "But Taurus, according to legend, *is* a minotaur, is he not?"

Virgil shook his head. "No, not quite. He's got the head of a bull and the torso of a man, but from the waist down, he's all bear."

Ruby and Bloom exchanged a glance, and Bloom said, "So he's a man-bear-bull." She paused. "Bull-man-bear?"

Virgil nodded like that wasn't at all a weird combination of things to be.

Bloom followed up. "And you're sure that the thing that attacked you fit that description?"

"Absolutely."

Ruby admired Bloom's ability to keep an even tone as she said, "It's just that sometimes it's difficult to make out all the details of something when it sneaks up on you and attacks, especially in the middle of the night."

"I understand that, and you make a good point. But the moon was nearly full, and in my bear form, my sight's great at night. Also, I saw the thing plain as day before it attacked me."

An eyebrow shooting up her forehead indicated that Bloom's interest was officially piqued. "You saw it plain as day? What, was it just standing there staring at you?"

Ruby imagined a man-bear-bull standing and waving like a fool, and she had to bite her lip to keep from laughing.

"Pretty much," Virgil said. "I saw it across the clearing, and it was staring right at me. Looked exactly like Taurus. And there's been talk among the sleuth lately about the legend rising again. So my mind went straight to that."

The sheriff shot Ruby a quick inquisitive glance before saying, "What do you mean, talk? What are people saying, and who's saying it?"

He reached up and rubbed the back of his neck. "Oh, everyone's been talking about it. I mean, we all knew about it growing up. It was a story our parents told us to keep us from running in the forest alone before we were of age. But lately, it's been coming up in conversation a lot more."

"How do people bring it into the conversation?"

He wobbled his head from side to side, "You know, just mentioning it. Joking about it. Someone at dinner the other night mentioned that it was about time for it to return. I admit, I didn't know about that part of the legend, but apparently Taurus rises every four hundred and forty-four years. And we're due for it this year." He paused, inspecting the women for a moment. "You don't believe any of this, do you?"

Ruby clenched her jaw so she didn't accidentally say, "No, but only because it's a big, steaming pile of unicorn swirls," and Sheriff Bloom, ever the diplomat, said, "I don't believe anything until I see evidence of it. Nothing personal. But this is all very interesting, and I plan on looking into it further."

"I guess that's all I can ask," he said. "Do you need anything else, or can I get back in there?"

Bloom frowned. "I think we're all set for now. You take care of yourself, Virgil. Stella Lytefoot can heal just about anything, but that's only if the infection doesn't get you first. She can work wonders, but she can't bring anyone back from the dead."

Virgil laughed nervously, but Ruby didn't miss his glance her way. So she added, "And I refuse to bring anyone back from the dead. I wouldn't test your luck."

Bloom rolled her eyes. "Come on, True. Let's get out of his fur."

They were well a ways down the mountain when Ruby broke the contemplative silence. "You'd think I would have come across the legend of Taurus in some of my reading."

"I was just thinking the same thing. I've never heard of it before. But then again, there are so many legends in each culture, it's hard to keep up. And parents will make up whatever stories they need to keep their children safe."

Ruby nearly second-guessed herself before asking, "Did yours?"

Bloom shot her a sideways glance. "I know what you're *really* asking. Not like you to be so coy."

"And not like you to avoid answering a simple question."

Bloom chuckled. "You couldn't find the answer in one of your books?"

"You know as well as I do that literature on angels is scarce at best."

"It's not by accident. My kind loves secrecy." She leaned close and whispered, "Helps preserve the mystique."

Ruby rolled her eyes, and Bloom added, "To answer your roundabout question, angels don't have parents."

"Then that leads to my next question: however do you manage to develop lifelong hang-ups, if not through parenting? Angel psychology must be terribly boring. Freud would have a heart attack if he knew."

The incline flattened out and they were finally back on a cobblestone road leading toward town. "I don't know who Freud is," Bloom said, "but if he enjoys issues, angels have plenty. Imagine being popped into existence fully grown and then abandoned by the goddess and left to fend for yourself. There's a reason I left Heaven first chance I got. The power struggle up there is relentless."

Ruby and Clifford shared a quick look. " 'Up there?' "

"Yep." Bloom nodded toward the clouds. "The gateway to the Heaven realm is always in the sky. That keeps the flightless riffraff from getting in."

Ruby ran through a quick inventory of species in her mind. "And what about the harpies and dragons?"

"If they get in, they don't stay long." Bloom sighed. "You get more than a few angels together and the egos are insufferable. So high and mighty. I got out as soon as I could."

Chapter Six

Following her departure from Bloom, Ruby had indulged herself and Clifford with so much beef stew from a bistro just off Fulcrum Park that she'd sidestepped Mirna the Overly Aggressive Spirit who was still anchored to the copper bowl on her parlor table, and gone straight upstairs to bed, where she'd slipped off to sleep the moment her head hit the pillow.

In fact, she slept so hard that she almost overslept the next morning. And indeed, when she did awake and glanced at the elven-made clock on the wall, she strongly questioned the necessity of her presence on Sheriff Bloom's morning errand.

But in the end, she knew that an hour more of sleep wasn't as valuable as what her Insight might gain from a chat with the minotaur Slobodan Yurosi.

She dressed in the same outfit as the day before, a custom that wasn't at all frowned upon in Eastwind due to the many magical ways of washing and the quality-

over-quantity   mindset   of   local   self-proclaimed
fashionistas.

She descended the stairs from her second-floor bedroom to the parlor and made straight for the bathroom (ignoring Mirna's verbal abuse) where she shuffled under the shower head, still fully clothed, and turned the handle. Rather than water, a shimmering flow of refreshing magic cascaded down and over her, not only lifting the grime from yesterday's clothes and rejuvenating her sleep-heavy skin, but also bringing her wavy bob of red hair to its peak volume without the frizz.

She approached the mirror to put the finishing touches on her look. There weren't many to do. She frowned slightly, noting that her red hair was looking awfully gray lately. Well, she supposed she should be grateful she had any of her color left at forty-six. But it wouldn't be long, she knew, until her whole head was white. Even her eyebrows and... other places... were turning up grays.

She sighed. Nobody said aging was a hoot. So in that sense, she couldn't blame Ezra for what he'd done...

"Sausage wraps on the way?" she called to Clifford as she exited the bathroom and slipped on her boots.

"You're too good to me."

"And you return the favor, my dear."

She patted him on the head as she passed. The hound had saved her hide more times than she could count, and while she'd never owned a pet before coming to Eastwind and had been concerned about the responsibility involved in having as interdependent (or co-dependent, if she were honest) of a relationship with one as a witch had with her familiar.

NOVA NELSON

But as it turned out, Clifford had been the best thing that had ever happened to her. She could be alone *with* him. It was the perfect balance of solitude and companionship, and after so many wonderful years, she wondered how she'd ever gotten by without him.

"Mirna," she said, addressing the scowling spirit, "why don't you give it a rest? Usually I'd sit with you and listen to your problems, talk you through them, maybe tie up a few loose ends for you in the physical world, and send you on your way, but unfortunately, something big has come up, and I like to focus on one thing at a time."

"Then focus on me," snapped the spirit. "You kidnapped me before all this started."

"Binding and kidnapping are not quite the same thing."

"Yes, they are."

"Okay, fine. They are. What are you going to do, call the sheriff on me?"

That only set the sprit into another rage spiral; Ruby was not looking forward to unraveling whatever knots were tethering this one to her old life. She considered simply banishing Mirna—it would only take a moment to do, and then the spirit would be out of her life forever—but she couldn't do that. Not even to Mirna. Banishment with unfinished business was a forever sentence to misery.

Later, strolling toward the sheriff's department, Ruby finished the last of her breakfast, tossing the wrapper into a nearby trashcan (Clifford had long finished his) and, shamelessly licking the grease off her fingers.

Gabby Bloom came marching up the street, cutting

easily through the sparse Thursday morning crowds and looking slightly frazzled but friendly nonetheless.

Without so much as a hello, the angel said, "Ready?" She held out a to-go cup of coffee, which Ruby accepted.

She stared down at the cup. "You know, I'm more of a tea drinker."

Bloom nodded. "I do. Which is why I'm giving you coffee. I need you a little over-caffeinated today."

"I thought we'd talked about this before. Coffee only makes me more blunt than usual."

"Exactly." Bloom nodded for Ruby and Clifford to follow her as she started down the road. "We're about to visit the residence of a minotaur. Have you ever spoken with a minotaur?"

Ruby considered it. "Not outside of casual interactions." They'd worked many cases together, but somehow minotaurs had never been involved. That spoke well of their kind, she decided.

"Then you're in for a treat." Bloom chuckled. "They might be even more blunt than you. And they appreciate the same level of communication in return."

As they began walking down the road, toward the outer edge of town, Ruby said, "Hmm... maybe I'm part minotaur."

"If you are, it's just the torso part. Unless you're hiding some hairy legs under those robes."

"Oh, I am, but it's all human hair."

"Human?" Bloom narrowed her eyes at Ruby.

"You know, like a witch, but with no magic or shifting abilities?... Never mind. And old-world thing. Suffice it to say there is no bull hair on me."

Slobodan Yurosi lived in the Ravenwood

neighborhood on the southwestern edge of town. His address was near enough to the Deadwoods for a convenient romp, but not so near that Ruby felt overly anxious going there.

Ravenwood was a neighborhood she was entirely unfamiliar with. There were only a handful of minotaurs in Eastwind, and from what Bloom told her on their walk, while Ruby sucked down her coffee, they were all gathered in that one neighborhood. That wasn't unusual. People liked to keep with their own for the most part. That could be observed all over Eastwind—while not everyone who lived in Erin Park was a leprechaun, every leprechaun Ruby had ever met lived in Erin Park. Same went for the werewolf aristocracy in Hightower Gardens... and the werewolf commoners in the Outskirts. However, the closer one got to the center of town, the more diverse each street became. Her home was only a few blocks away from the heart, for instance, and the other three cottages on her row housed a family of fauns, a young but starry-eyed werewolf-pixie couple, and an elf who looked to be about thirty but was likely closer to one hundred and ten. Even though Ruby left her house infrequently, she preferred to see a variety of creatures and classes when she did so. Get too many people of a similar background together, and things tended to get a little hostile for everyone else. And because there was no one like her in town, she had to pay attention to that sort of hostility and avoid it wherever possible.

Besides the minotaurs, Ravenwood was home to most of Eastwind's less welcome creatures—goblins, ogres, and even a few former Deadwoods inhabitants who were run out of their homes.

She was surprised to find that Ravenwood even had its own neighborhood square that seemed to carry most of the essentials, presumably so those in this neighborhood didn't have to venture more centrally and subject themselves to the scorn and suspicion of others.

She could relate. Perhaps she should have settled in Ravenwood.

The garden outside Slobodan's home only had a few bristly shrubs protruding from a landscape of tiny pebbles. Bloom led the way up the sidewalk to the front door and knocked authoritatively. "Mr. Yurosi? It's Sheriff Bloom."

The door opened a few minutes later, and Slobodan's dark bull eyes stared out from the dim interior. Ruby hated to judge creatures for the things they couldn't control, but she always found it disconcerting to come face-to-face with a minotaur. They generally wore clothes according to Eastwind custom, meaning they didn't just walk around bare-chested all the time. And they could have been mistaken for just any old witch if it weren't for, you know, the bull's head and large, dangerous horns. She would never *not* find it strange to hear the voice of a human coming from the lips of a bull.

Slobodan met Gabby's gaze confidently, but said nothing until he looked at Ruby then back to the sheriff. "Why is *she* here?"

"*Your reputation precedes you again,*" Clifford grumbled.

"*I'm sure your presence provides a helpful context clue.*"

"She's helping me with the investigation," Bloom replied.

"You said in your letter that this was regarding a missing person. How could a Fifth Wind help if no one is dead?" Bloom had described minotaurs as blunt, but Ruby was quite liking the way he cut straight to the point.

"Fifth Winds have the gift of Insight. Even if no one is dead, she provides a smart second opinion to my observations."

He nodded curtly, only once. "The hound stays outside."

Ruby straightened her spine. "No. The hound comes inside. He goes wherever I go."

Slobodan's eyes gave only the faintest hint of consideration before he said. "Is he house trained?"

"Of course he is."

"Then he may enter." He turned and walked inside, not bothering to hold the door for them.

"Glad I gave you that coffee," muttered Bloom.

"Oh, don't flatter yourself. I would have said that no matter what."

Careful where she stepped on the uneven flagstone floors, Ruby followed the sheriff inside, Clifford hot on her heels. He shut the door behind him with a big, heavy paw.

Slobodan led them into a large space that, not unlike Ruby's own home, contained the seating area, dining table, and kitchen. Utilitarian didn't even begin to cover his design style. "Ascetic" might have been closer. But "harsh" would have been even more on the nose. There were no pictures on the wall—there was nothing on any of the walls as far as Ruby could see—and there wasn't even a rug in front of the hearth.

"My wife will make you hot drinks if you demand it," he said, taking one of the four seats at the table. "She's upstairs mending a hole in the wall. I can call to her."

"What's the hole from?" Ruby asked.

"Anger."

Ruby looked at Bloom to see if this was something they should be follow up on, but the angel seemed unconcerned. She pulled out a chair and took a seat, so Ruby followed suit.

"We don't demand hot drinks," she said. "We only want to talk to you."

"Ask me your questions." He exhaled and Ruby could have sworn she could see the humid air swirl out of his bovine nostrils.

Bloom went ahead. "You're the chargehead of the Eastwind minotaurs, correct?"

"Yes."

"And you keep track of where your people run?"

"Yes."

"And you're sure they tell the truth about it?"

"None among the charge lie to me." He raised his chin slightly.

"Good to know. Have any of your people been on Fluke Mountain in the last few weeks? Specifically around the Silent Reach?"

"No. They prefer the Deadwoods and I specifically forbade them from running anywhere else. So few understand how my kind choose to live our lives, it's best if we keep to ourselves. The things that happen within the confines of the Deadwoods rarely pass through the lips of those who enter and survive to tell about it."

"So, none of your charge have entered the Silent Reach?"

"That is what I have told you already."

Bloom nodded. "And what do you know of Taurus?"

Slobodan clearly needed no time to consider it. "It is a false tale. A fabrication used by many weres to scare their children, and one woven at the expense of minotaur dignity."

"Do you know the tale?"

"Only vaguely, but it varies from teller to teller. The version I have heard most frequently goes like this. Taurus was the greatest of the minotaurs in Wisconsin."

Ruby jumped in. "Wisconsin?" That couldn't be right. "As in dairy farms and the Packers?"

Slobodan stared at her like she had just spoken complete gibberish. And to Ruby's discomfort, Sheriff Bloom's expression was similar.

Okay. Something had clearly been lost in translation. This used to happen all the time, but as she'd expanded her reading hours and simply spent more time learning through cultural osmosis, the occurrences had become more and more infrequent. Thankfully, she knew the best approach to take when something like this happened.

"How about you just tell me what Wisconsin means to you?" she said.

He'd said Wisconsin, though. She was sure of it. Wasn't she?

"Wisconsin is one of the many realms branching off from Avalon," Slobodan replied. "It is the original home of the weres. It is a land of wilderness and carnal luxuries. It is not the true home of minotaurs, but it is where we settled thousands of years ago when we were displaced from our world of origin."

"Ah," said Ruby. "Okay." She was only able to wonder briefly if the Wisconsin she knew had been at all influenced by creatures from the Wisconsin of which Slobodan spoke, or if the shared name was purely a coincidence of letters, before Bloom said, "Go on. Tell us more about Taurus."

"Taurus was a great leader. He ruled justly over the largest charge in minotaur history. When war in our homeland of Creton became too bloody and brutal, he led our people to new lands. He is said to have been not only a great leader but a fierce protector, and he was the one who first discovered the doorway to Wisconsin. Through it, he saw a land of hope, a place where minotaurs could be safe and flourish.

"But the legend says that the weres did not take kindly to our appearance, and even more vicious fighting ensued. When Taurus's lover was killed at the hands of a werebear, he vowed to kill every last were he could find until his dying day. He abandoned his protective care of the minotaurs, who were then forced to disburse through many worlds to seek shelter, and pursued his vengeance until his last breath. And with that last breath, he pledged to rise again, this time stronger than before, because not even Death could defeat him for long. And when he did rise, he would continue his slaughter until the moon and sun collided in the sky.

"That is how it goes," Slobodan concluded. "Of course, is it false."

"You don't believe there's any truth in it?" asked

Bloom. "Usually rumors and legends are based off of some shred of truth."

"The only truth is the treatment of my people by werekind. It has always been cruel. But the rest is false. It must be because it happened in a time before history. And nothing can overcome Death."

Ruby decided not to debate him on the issue and kept her mouth shut.

"So," Bloom said, "Taurus is just a minotaur?"

"Taurus is not real."

"No, I understand that, but I'm talking about in the story. Taurus is just a regular, if especially strong and vicious, minotaur?"

"Yes."

Bloom turned her full attention to Ruby. "The resurrection thing checks out at least." Then she stood from her chair and Ruby did the same.

Clifford, who'd been sitting attentively by Ruby's side and whose keen eyes had never left Slobodan, stood as well.

"Would it please you if I walked you to the door?" Slobodan asked without standing.

"Nope," said Bloom, already making her way out of the room. "Thank you for your time," she called over her shoulder.

And the minotaur replied, "I had no choice."

Ruby chuckled. "He's got a point."

Once they were outside, Bloom sighed. "I told you minotaurs made for strange conversation."

"I liked him," replied Ruby as they walked down the sidewalk toward the narrow street. "In fact, I might have loved him."

"Blunt, unromantic, house like an old crypt—he definitely seems more your type."

"Than?"

"Zax."

Ruby scoffed.

"And Ezra."

"Ah, well anyone who's aging normally is more my type than him."

"Quinn Shaw is newly single and aging quite nicely. Should I tell him to call on you?"

Ruby shrugged, trying not to let the thought of the uptight leprechaun showing up on her doorstep with flowers annoy her. "At least he's just about my height."

Bloom glanced down at her. "Oh please, you have at least a foot on him."

"I've always wanted to feel tall." She looked around at the changing architecture. They were getting closer to town. "Where are we off to now?"

"The library."

"Twist my arm, why don't you? And what are we looking for?"

"Taurus."

"Taurus, Taurus, *Taurus*. It's all we ever talk about anymore." She grunted. "And it's all just a load of bull."

Chapter Seven

Helena appeared about as irked as usual when Ruby called to her from the other side of the librarian's desk. But when the elf looked up from her book and saw Gabby Bloom in full uniform, she bothered to set her reading to the side and stand. "Can I help you?" she asked, her tone sweet like poisoned honey.

Bloom smiled congenially. "Yes, I'm hoping you can direct me to any information you might have on Taurus."

Helena arched an eyebrow and appeared delighted. "Taurus?"

"The minotaur, yes."

And now the elf narrowed her eyes at the sheriff. "There's only one reference to it that I know of. Very few people bother to write down every werebeast superstition. It would take an army of scribes centuries to do it, and by the time they finished, more superstitions would have been born from ignorance."

"Yes," said Bloom, only the slightest edge of impatience in her voice, "I understand that. Regardless, I would love if you could direct me to that single reference."

Helena shrugged. "It's your time wasted." She pointed to a row of shelves on the far side of the room. "It would be in our creature section. I believe it's in volume three of *A Wealth of Werebears*."

Bloom thanked the librarian and led the way over to the shelf. Ruby was well acquainted with this section, having spent many hours in it during her first few years in town, versing herself with all the many types of beings she might encounter both in this life and the next.

Because she was the first Fifth Wind witch Eastwind had seen in many, many years, she'd had no one to guide her and was forced to read book after book to get her feet under her. Thankfully, learning had always been her preferred method for passing the time. But unfortunately, it seemed like no matter how much she'd read, she was still behind. Wisconsin, for instance. How had she not heard of that realm before? Or maybe she had early on, and her aging mind had already forgotten it.

No, she wouldn't go down that road.

She sidestepped quickly and narrowly avoided taking a heavy floating book to the abdomen. "Watch where you're going," she snapped at the distracted spirit.

He looked up, saw that Ruby was staring directly at him, blinked a few times, and then scurried off, disappearing down one of the dark tunnels leading off from the bright and spacious atrium.

Bloom located the book without much searching among the shelves and flipped it open. This was by no means their first trip to the library together, and while Ruby did love to read, Bloom's hundreds (thousands?) of years of experience made her a speed reader to be reckoned with, so Ruby let her take the lead whenever it came up.

"Hmm..." said Bloom, her eyes still soaring over the words. She flipped the page and said "hmm..." again.

"Care to enlighten me?"

Bloom held up a finger to silence Ruby, then used that same finger to flip the page again. Then she flipped back to the previous page. "Hmm..."

"Oh, come out with it!"

Finally, Bloom looked up, the large musty book still open in her left hand. "There's just a brief mention of Taurus here. Maybe there's more farther on. I'll check in a second."

"And what does it say?"

Bloom read it off. "Because of their directness and minimal desire for rich social interactions, minotaurs have frequently become objectified within werekind's myths, often employed as a symbol of death and destruction or a dangerous adversary. The legend of Taurus, for example, is passed down through various werebeast cultures and is generally used as a means to keep their young from venturing out on their own."

Ruby waited for more, but Bloom had stopped speaking. "That's it?"

"In this section, yes. I thought it might continue on the next page, but it changes topic completely. Give me a few minutes, and I'll finish the rest of this one and let you know what I find."

Ruby nodded and decided there was no point in hovering. She tucked her hands into the pockets of her long robes and nodded for Clifford to follow on their stroll.

They passed a smattering of Eastwinders whom Ruby only vaguely recognized sitting at the long reading tables.

"I've been here twenty years and there are still so many people I don't know. It's not a large town."

"Eighteen hundred and twenty-seven," replied Clifford.

"What's that?"

"The population. Although, depending on how this Swamy thing shakes out, it could be eighteen hundred and twenty-six."

A young ogre who could have been mistaken for a boulder sat completely still, hunched over a thick book with its black leather cover peeking out around the edges of the pages. On the table beside it were no fewer than a dozen other books stacked precariously one on top of the other. A hard nudge to the table, and they would have come tumbling down.

Ruby had a strong urge to ask the young ogre if he should be in school, but she supposed any child who skipped school to go read at the library would probably be better off in the long run.

Was Bloom done yet? It wasn't like Ruby to be anything but relaxed at the library, but she knew she didn't have enough time to dive into a book on her own, so she felt a little like a kid in a candy store without any money.

Well, it wouldn't hurt to browse. Maybe she could find something else to read once she got through the ten she already had at home.

She knew a shortcut through the rows of physical enchantment manuals toward the fiction section (her favorite), but she hardly made it around the first corner before she nearly smacked right into a face she *could* put a name to.

"Oh, pardon!" She blinked. "Ezra."

He looked up from the book in his hands and grinned. "Ruby!" His smooth, dark skin and eyes as sweet and rich as chocolate sucked her in and transported her back in time. That was always the case when she saw him because he existed outside of time, and had for almost fifteen years now, not aging a single day... as her red hair took on more and more grays.

He'd had a choice about it. It wasn't as if someone had cursed him with youth. And in the end, he'd made his choice, and a life with her, growing slowly older together, wasn't the life the South Wind witch had chosen.

He snapped the book shut and slid it back on the shelf, but not before she glimpsed the title on the spine. *Amulets for the Ages: Appropriate Protection for Young Witches.*

"How are you, my beautiful lady?" he asked.

Surely, he must have known calling her beautiful after everything that'd happened would only made her angry.

But, no. She wouldn't take it personally. Ezra was like this to everyone. His incredible levels of charisma and unparalleled likability were what allowed him to simply stop the aging process midway through his thirties and have not a single person in Eastwind decide to look into what was going on behind the scenes. Everyone had turned a blind eye, perhaps because they were just thrilled to think they could have him around town longer. Did it work that way? Had be become an actual immortal?

She'd never bothered to ask, because it was no longer relevant to her.

She brushed off his initial question, and said, "Thinking of creating a new product?" She nodded toward the book.

"Ah yes." He held it up demonstratively, beaming. "I had a concerned mother come into the store yesterday asking about protection for her young twins. She seemed convinced her house was haunted."

Ruby groaned. "That woman didn't happen to be Mrs. Goldhorn, did it?"

Ezra's pleasant smile didn't falter, but he did tilt his head to the side. "It did. How'd you know?"

"She consulted me on the matter. I told her it wasn't a ghost she was dealing with but rather the twins themselves who were hiding things around her house. Guess she wanted it to be a ghost badly enough to ignore the wisdom of the person in town who would actually know."

Ezra chuckled. "You know everyone around here is dying for a good story."

"I do, but I don't understand it. With all the fangs and claws, we're only ever a few seconds away from a deadly altercation."

Ezra tucked the book under one arm and slipped his hands into his pants pockets, leaning a shoulder against the sturdy bookshelf. "It's true."

"I suppose you'll still settle on some new amulets for

children?"

"Naturally. It's not my job to sell people like Mrs. Goldhorn the truth. It's my job to sell them what they want. And if people want a protective amulet for babies—who you and I both know are notoriously poor vessels for any type of possession—then it's my job to stock them."

"A crystal neckless is more dangerous for a toddler than any spirit could be."

"Which is why I'm looking for other ways to charm the wee ones that won't accidentally snuff them out."

"You're such a hero," she quipped.

Clifford stepped forward, wagging his tail lazily, and Ruby thought *traitor* just before Ezra's grin stretched wide and he scratched the hellhound behind the ears. "Good to see you, friend," Ezra said. Clifford's nose went to his pocket, and the witch chuckled, jammed a hand inside, and pulled out a small parcel. He unwrapped the cloth to reveal a few small cookies. "I could never sneak this by you, my man." He offered one of the cookies to Clifford, who took it happily.

"And you?" Ezra said, offering them to Ruby.

They did look delicious, but she found she wasn't in the mood to take anything from him right now. In fact, his generosity and usual charm was suddenly more irritating than she could stand.

"No, thank you," she said, keeping her voice level. "I can't just eat whatever I want anymore. I'm not as young as I used to be."

The silence between them was nothing short of icy, and she regretted her harsh jab as soon as she'd said it. Because a part of her completely understood why Ezra had made the decision he had. He'd done what every mortal wished they could do. And it wasn't like he hadn't offered Ruby the same thing. They could have stayed just like they were back then, together...

And she'd chosen not to. They'd both made a choice.

But before she could apologize for the unnecessary punch below the belt and assure him it was all water under the bridge and she didn't know what had gotten into her, Bloom's voice cut through the tension like a knife. "There you are. Ah! And Ezra! How are you, sir?"

He nodded and grinned at the angel in such a convincing way that Ruby wondered if she'd simply imagined the hurt expression he'd donned just a moment before. Maybe she'd only seen what she'd wanted to see.

"I'm doing fantastic, Sheriff. Just a little research for the store, and I had the treat of running into Ruby and Cliff. I had no idea when I woke up this morning that it would be my lucky day."

Not even Bloom was immune to his charms, and she chuckled in a manner that bordered disconcertingly on a giggle. "I hope you'll excuse Ruby. I need to speak with her."

"Ooh..." He leaned forward conspiratorially. "Official business?"

"Is it ever not?" said Bloom.

"Not with you, Gabby. You could ride a unicorn across town in nothing but the skin your goddess gave you, call it official business, and I would argue to my grave that it was."

Ruby's eyes went wide, and she turned to the sheriff, expecting his words to be taken with at least a little offense. After all, Bloom was nothing if not stately, classy, and respectable, so—

.ne angel *blushing*?

.oy observed with more than a little shock that she
. And it only made the sheriff even more
.ighteningly beautiful.

"Oh hush," Bloom said, and by this point, Ruby was actually surprised the sheriff didn't take a playful swat at him.

"We'd better get back to work," Ruby cut in. Then she grabbed Bloom by the arm and without another word to Ezra, pulled the sheriff away.

Once they had some distance between them and the South Wind, Bloom slipped her arm free from Ruby's grasp. "Sorry," she said. "I hope I didn't make you... I just mean, I didn't intend to interrupt."

"You didn't interrupt, and you didn't make me jealous. If anything, you made me feel a little better about how easily I can slip back into it with him."

"He's charming, that's for sure."

"Emphasis on charm. If anyone's found a magical way to conjure that sort of charisma, it's Ezra."

Bloom sighed. "You know, he once sold me a pocket crystal that helps improve judgment."

Ruby shook her head. "I can believe it. He could sell... well, he could sell a judgment crystal to an angel. That's about the most ridiculous thing I could think of."

Bloom led the way toward the exist, and Ruby chimed in with, "I suppose you got all you needed from the book?"

"I did. There was nothing else on Taurus. Not in that one or the other two volumes. I even looked through one on Minotaur folklore and found just one mention that was about as informative as the first."

"So where are we headed now?"

"I'm headed back to the sheriff's department. You're free to head home for now. I think it's pretty clear there's nothing to this tale of Taurus."

"It wasn't clear to you before?"

They entered into the bright spring day and Ruby shielded her eyes from the sun. Bloom didn't seem to notice it. "It was clear enough, but I don't like to rule anything out, no matter how far-fetched it sounds. And now I can confidently tell anyone who mentions it that the creature they speak of is complete unicorn swirls."

"So, what do you think we're dealing with?"

Bloom paused and put her hands on her hips, looking down at Ruby. "I don't really know. That's another thing I just learned. Minotaur scratches are necrotic."

"Meaning?"

"Meaning you don't want them. It takes quite a powerful treatment to keep the skin around the wounds from rotting and falling off. A minotaur scratches you on your calf, and you could end up losing your whole leg if you're not careful."

"Were Virgil's injuries like that?"

Bloom shrugged. "That's what we don't know. I didn't know about the necrosis at the time, so I didn't think to check under the bandages."

"That says a lot about minotaur restraint, if you've never had need to know."

"It does. But I guess they've learned their lesson after being run out of every place they've ever settled. Wish witches were as quick of learners." She snuck a sideways glance at Ruby.

"What?" said the Fifth Wind, "I don't disagree with

you. Witches don't make good neighbors."

"Don't forget you're one of them."

Ruby scoffed. "I wouldn't dare. Don't tell any of *them* that. They'd much rather forget."

Her mind wandered for only a minute before it traveled back to the topic at hand. "Zax was getting supplies at the Pixie Mixie for Virgil's wounds. You think that means the injury is necrotic or not?"

The sheriff narrowed her eyes thoughtfully. "Did he by any chance buy phoenix blood?"

"Phoenix blood?" said Ruby, surprised. "Do they even sell that at the Pixie Mixie?"

"They do, but it's kept behind lock and key. They have to import it from Avalon, so it's not cheap."

"I don't think I saw him buy anything like that, but I wasn't exactly keeping tabs on his shopping basket."

Bloom fell silent. Then, when it seemed like she might be done with the conversation, she said, "I'll go check on Virgil once I speak with Deputy Titterfield and see about this morning's search party. If Virgil's wounds are healing just fine, then we don't have a minotaur on our hands."

"And we're agreed that it's not Taurus we're dealing with?"

Bloom nodded. "Yes, we're in agreement on that."

"Well then. You better get back to your official business, and I'm going to attend to mine."

"Which is?"

"A nap. Not all of us have the energy to ride a unicorn naked through town, you know."

Bloom shook her head, and the two women parted ways.

Chapter Eight

Sheriff Bloom wasn't sure what to make of this strange case so far. She sat in her office, surrounded by the familiar stacks of unfinished paperwork for the High Council, and contemplated the facts.

Often, when she could take a minute to herself and run through each fact one by one, turning it over and examining it, tuning into her innate gift of judgment to see if she could draw anything to the surface, she would discover that a fundamental assumption she'd been carrying with her was flawed. Things usually fell into place after that. At least they had for the hundreds of years since she'd taken this job in Eastwind.

Fact number one: Swamy was missing. Or at least Opal didn't seem to know where he was. Those two things, though, were not necessarily the same. And it was important to keep that in mind.

Often, when people went missing, they were either on the run from something dangerous, were already dead, or had simply gone on a trip and forgotten to leave notice.

Only a couple of times had people *actually* gone missing in Eastwind to the point where even the missing person didn't know where he or she was. That usually involved a Befuddlement Brew or some other form of disorientation magic, though. So far, there were no signs of magical interference, but she would keep an eye out for it.

Fact number two: something had attacked Virgil in the woods.

But could she be sure of that? She hadn't actually seen his scratches. She'd only seen a bandage. She'd taken Zax's word for it that there had been scratches, but either he could be lying or Virgil could have managed to mislead him. Or even stranger, Virgil could have self-inflicted scratches. She had just as much evidence for one theory as she did the next, when it came down to it.

Fact number three: Virgil saw something that looked like a minotaur in the woods of the Silent Reach.

Again, he could be lying. Or he could simply be mistaken. That was one of the many interesting inconsistencies when people were attacked. Some were able to recall every vivid detail of the attacker, from eye color to his smell to a single misaligned tooth, or even freckle patterns—but those same people couldn't tell you a single thing about anything else in their surroundings. Meanwhile, other victims were shown to be so far off on their attacker's description that they might point the finger at a genie when the assailant was actually a leprechaun. But victims in that second group *could* provide a vivid and accurate account of the environment —a leaky faucet in the next room over from the attack or a unique plant that they'd almost fallen on when they were tackled.

The trick for Bloom was figuring out which kind of witness each victim was. Memories were fickle things. They wanted nothing more than to be whole, and that usually meant making up details to fill in the gaps. Memories also wanted to serve the rememberer, and that could lead to the mind erasing the worst of the ordeal and whitewashing it with something tolerable.

Bloom sighed and tried to recall more assumed facts she'd been holding onto, whether consciously or subconsciously, in her investigation thus far, but her focus for the day was waning, and the immensity of the paperwork around her, which she may never get through in all her immortal years, came crashing through her awareness, demanding to be seen.

"Fine," she muttered, and took one of the reports from the top of a stack and began looking it over. Goddess save her, this one was from two years ago. Deputy Titterfield had written it up in his usual scrawl and all she had to do was read it over, sign it, and file it away in the departmental records cavern below the station.

It was tempting to sign it without reading it—after all, what were the odds that anyone on the High Council was actually looking these over?—but her conscience wouldn't let her.

Stupid conscience. I bet Ruby wouldn't have a problem just signing the form.

She'd hardly put a dent in the pile, relocating each finished form to the records department with a flick of her wrist and feeling a small high as it disappeared, when there was a knock on her office door.

"Come in."

The door opened and Deputy Titterfield peeked his head in. "Afternoon, Sheriff."

"Afternoon. What's the latest?"

Deputy Titterfield had been on the force for decades. As the only deputy in the Eastwind Sheriff's Department, he was usually all that stood between order and chaos in the town while she was cooped up in the office. He did as well of a job as she could expect any single person to do, but he was getting up there in years, and so she'd found herself forced to step out of the office and be more hands-on than usual lately. She didn't mind it one bit. The paperwork, on the other hand, seemed to be holding a grudge.

Morris Titterfield had been a good deputy from day one. Not great, but good. Yet he was a North Wind witch, not an immortal or even a long-lifer, and the years were wearing on him now.

"We completed the first sweep of the Silent Reach. No sign of Mr. Stormstruck. I have the volunteers searching everything within a mile radius of the edge of the Reach. We should be able to complete that by nightfall. If we can't find anything, we widen the search by a mile in each direction tomorrow, starting at sunrise."

Only once Bloom heard the news did she realize she'd been expecting as much. "Complete today's plans, otherwise the volunteers will start spreading rumors around town that we've already given him up for dead. But then send word to volunteers in the morning that we've gotten another lead and are taking the investigation in another direction. They'll just be so glad they aren't expected to go back out first thing, they won't question it."

Titterfield nodded. "And do we have another lead?"

"Not yet," Bloom said. "But I have faith another one will be coming very soon."

"What makes you say that?"

"Because this is usually the point in the investigation when those who know more than they're letting on get antsy and make a foolish move."

Titterfield's grin hardly turned the corner of his lips, but it was there. "Whatever you say, Sheriff."

He nodded and made to step out of her office, but Bloom called after him. "Morris." He paused, his eyebrows raising at her use of his first name. "Find a volunteer to lead the rest of the day's search, and then go home and get some rest."

"Yes, Sheriff."

He shut the door behind him and Bloom felt back into thought.

While she knew in her heart that what she'd said about another lead showing up was true, there was always that part of her that doubted it would happen, that this time might be the exception.

That was the way it always was, though. Faith didn't exist without doubt.

But, good goddess, were they maddening bedfellows.

Chapter Nine

Ruby's nap had been fitful at best, and non-existent at worst. At one point, she was pretty sure she'd slept, simply because her mind had spun a strange movie that involved Sheriff Bloom riding Taurus through town (fully clothed, thankfully), while Ezra and Zax juggled three kids (the faun variety) between them.

Clifford's snoring had finally tugged her from that dream or reverie or (goddess forbid) vision and she'd been grateful for it. There was something she was missing in all this, so she'd decided to be a bit more purposeful about summoning her subconscious to her.

She pulled on a robe and stuffed her swollen feet into her slippers. The swelling was a new perk of growing older, brought on by any walk in her boots along the cobblestone streets that lasted longer than twenty minutes, which were most walks through town. She was sure there was a tincture of some kind at the Pixie Mixie that would cure this new condition, but that would require her admitting to herself that it wasn't just a fluke, that her body really was irreversibly falling apart.

She hadn't yet been ready to make that concession in any monetary way.

But as she limped down the stairs, she thought she might be ready to make that concession in the morning.

Clifford didn't bother getting up from his padded bed on her bedroom floor, which was fine. She didn't need him for what she was about to do.

Once back downstairs in her parlor, she threatened Mirna with banishment until the spirit temporarily faded out of sight and sound, and then she settled herself in the overstuffed chair by the fire. It was the same chair Ezra had imported for her from Avalon years ago because he knew she would like the particular shade of violet and her old reading chair had been an unforgiving wooden rocker. He had been right. She loved her chair.

She forced all thought of that witch from her mind and shut her eyes. Her gift of Insight could be fickle, but she'd grown more in control of it year after year. It'd been a good two years of being in Eastwind before she even stumbled over the *concept* of it in a book and realized that Insight was the greatest strength of Fifth Winds. Could have saved her a lot of trouble in her early years if she'd known to trust her gut more, but she supposed that could be said for almost anyone. And weren't one's twenties for making comically poor decisions with an unholy degree of certainty that one was making the correct choice?

But now she was fairly sure she'd read every book in the library that so much as mentioned the word "Insight," and she was glad she had. It proved invaluable in times like these.

What had once felt little more than a tickle in the back of her mind and a slight twinge in her core, had blossomed into a wealth of wisdom she could access under the right circumstances. While it felt like magic, she was fairly sure Insight fell more under the heading of logic. She felt it in her gut, sure, but it lived and breathed in her mind.

Because, when it came down to it, her Insight never told her anything she didn't already know. It just pointed her in the right direction, and made connections between seemingly disparate things she'd forgotten she knew.

She twisted in her seat and pulled the patchwork quilt off the back of her chair, draping it over her legs to help settle her nervous system. And then she shut her eyes and focused on her breathing.

Once she'd found a comfortable rhythm, she asked her question. *What am I missing?*

It was minutes before the image appeared. But there it was: a figure with the legs of a bear, the torso of a man, and the head of a bull. He stood in a clearing at night with moonlight glowing around him. He stood staring at her, his arms out by his side, his human fingers bent like claws, his chest heaving.

And then he charged.

Ruby yelped when someone pounded at her front door, giving her meditative whiplash.

Clifford stampeded down the stairwell, yelling, *"Someone's here. Who is it? Who is it? Who is it? I'll take care of it!"*

To anyone but Ruby, it would simply sound like deep, hellacious barking, but she hardly noticed that part.

"Calm down," she said. "I'm sure it's fine."

But she wasn't sure it was fine. Whether that was because the image of Taurus charging had rattled her nerves or because her Insight was still whispering to her, she couldn't be certain.

So when Clifford stayed glued to her side as she went to answer the door, she didn't tell him no.

She wasn't sure who she was expecting to see, but if it'd been Bloom or even Ezra, she wouldn't have been surprised.

It was neither of them.

Instead, two werebears smiled nervously at her. "Can we come in?" Opal Barker asked.

Ruby's eyes traveled from her to the man next to her, who looked uncannily like Virgil Pine, though he stood half a foot taller and seemed to have a handful of years on him. "And you are?"

"Cedric Pine."

"Virgil's brother."

He nodded.

"Oh, all right then, come on in." She stepped aside and let them pass, but didn't miss Clifford's close inspection of them via trained sniffer.

Cedric was tall enough that he had to crouch slightly to avoid hitting his head on the assortment of dangling wards Ruby hung from the parlor ceiling. He eyed them suspiciously.

"Don't mind them. They're all positive. Well, except that one." She pointed to a mobile made entirely of petrified bats. "But I hardly ever tap into that one. It's mostly there for decoration." Opal and Cedric shared a quick nervous glance, and Ruby added, "Sit, please. I'll make some tea."

The offer calmed them as she'd intended it to, and she allowed them a moment to take in the novel space while she put the kettle on and spooned out a mixture of tea leaves that included chamomile, lavender, and a little bit of slippery elm (to loosen their tongues). Thankfully, you could hardly taste or smell the last ingredient over the soothing scent of the others.

When she returned to the table with the tea tray and began serving each of them, she smiled and said, "I assume you know something regarding Swamy's disappearance that you'd like to share."

She poured the last cup then folded her hands in her lap, waiting patiently.

Neither of her guests spoke. But she did notice that Opal's hands were shaking. Ruby nodded at her shaking hands. "The tea will help with that. But I suspect telling me why you're here will as well."

"We saw him," Opal said quickly.

Ruby sat up straighter. "Swamy?"

"No. Not Swamy. Taurus."

Ruby's eyes flickered to Cedric as she tried to gauge whether this was a joke. He seemed embarrassed, but not the kind one feels from pulling a lame prank.

For fang's sake... They seemed to be telling the truth. Or at least what they believed to be truth. She'd read about group hallucinations before. Could it be something like that? Perhaps someone was casting an enchantment over Fluke Mountain.

"You saw Taurus?" she prompted, trying not to sound as judgmental as she felt.

Opal nodded. "Outside the lodge. I saw him through

a window in the restaurant's kitchen. Or at least, I thought I did."

Cedric took over. "She mentioned it to me and I went outside to look. I saw him, too, but only briefly as he was running away."

Yes, they seemed serious enough. Ruby looked at the clock on her wall. It was nearly one in the morning. From what she remembered of the restaurant hours posted on a small sign by the host stand, it closed at ten each night. She began doing the math of how long the last diners might stay, added in time to clean and close the kitchen and the walk from Fluke Mountain to her house.

The timeline was feasible, but still a stretch.

"What time did you see Taurus?" she asked.

Cedric opened his mouth, but Opal jumped in. "Just after close."

"I'm unfamiliar with your hours," Ruby lied. "What time is close?"

"Nine."

Oh, so even earlier than she'd thought. "Were there still diners around when you saw it?"

Opal's eyes fell to her cup of tea, and she cradled it between her palms. "No, I believe the last couple had left a few minutes before."

"So, no one else to corroborate your story?"

And now Opal looked up from the surface of her drink, and her eyes cut into Ruby. "You don't believe us?"

"I don't know what to believe. Trust me, my job would be much easier if everyone told the truth all the time and I never ran into stories about legends coming to life, but alas, that's not the case. So I must practice skepticism. I hope you'll forgive me once it gets to the bottom of your boyfriend's disappearance."

That did it. The werebear looked properly embarrassed and didn't respond.

"Now," Ruby began, addressing Cedric to test for holes in his story, "would you describe what Taurus looked like?"

Cedric nodded and shrugged his hefty shoulders. "Just like you would expect."

"Begging your forgiveness, but I don't have any expectations of his appearance at all. Could you be more specific?"

He took a deep breath, leaned back in his chair, and stared vaguely toward the baubles on the ceiling. "Bull's head, with big horns, like a minotaur. Bare chest like a man's. From just below, oh, maybe the belly button down, he looked like a werebear. Big, thick legs with brown fur."

"And you were able to see the color of his fur in the darkness?"

Cedric nodded nonchalantly, like that was obvious.

"Were you in your bear form?"

"No."

"Was he in moonlight?"

"No, it was mostly shadows." He sat up straighter, and his voice deepened. "But I know what I saw."

She smiled softly. "No need to get worked up, just trying to get the facts." But now it was clear that he didn't know what he'd seen. If he wasn't in his bear form, then his eyes were limited like hers. She'd once read in an obscure book on were anatomy that the number of rods and cones in a were's eyes shifted along with his or her form. That meant that werebears had just as poor night vision as she did when they weren't full-on hairy.

But more importantly, it also meant that they couldn't see colors at night.

It was a strange phenomenon and one she hadn't considered herself until the library book had brought it up. But while someone with her optical anatomy could make out shapes and movement in the darkness, thanks to the rods in one's eyes, the cones, which detect color, were all but useless in such conditions. Which meant that whatever color one might "see" in the nighttime was only a mental projection based upon past data. One can't tell a tree is green at night, but the brain assures you that it always has been and therefore still is, so your mind colors it in.

It all amounted to the fact that Cedric wasn't an especially reliable witness. He couldn't have *seen* the brown fur. He could have seen fur, but his assumption that it was brown came from somewhere else. Perhaps the myths circulating around the werebear sleuth had mentioned that fact. Or maybe his brother had dropped the detail into his story of the attack. Either way, Cedric didn't seem keen on a simple "I don't know" to her questions, and was happy to fill in the details as needed without questioning where the information had originated. He was a tainted witness, in other words.

She addressed her next question to him. "Do you believe Taurus has anything to do with Swamy's disappearance?"

He nodded adamantly. "Absolutely. The timing is too coincidental."

"But we don't have a body, as far as I know." She

hadn't spoken to Bloom since the search party was due to wrap up, but she assumed she would have heard an owl pecking at her bedroom window with an urgent message from the sheriff, if anything had turned up.

"Doesn't mean anything," Cedric replied. "He could have been mauled and dragged off somewhere."

Ruby checked on Opal's expression, and it seemed vague and faraway.

"Was Taurus so large as to manage such a feat? From the pictures I've seen of Swamy, he's not a small bear. It would take quite a creature to overpower him and drag him off."

Cedric nodded his understanding. "Taurus was huge. Easily a foot taller than Swamy. And his arms were thick as ancient oaks."

Opal nodded emphatically now, despite the obvious exaggeration, then took a long sip of her tea and seemed to relax.

"Ah yes," said Ruby. "Drink up. It will help settle the nerves."

They both did, and Ruby simply brought hers up to her nose and inhaled deeply. The scent alone helped to still the many swirling half-formed thoughts in her mind.

"For what it's worth," she said. "I believe you're telling me the truth." She refrained from mentioning that she thought their truth could be completely false.

Both werebears appeared greatly relieved, which was exactly how she'd wanted them to feel before asking the next question. "Why did you come to me about this instead of, say, the sheriff?"

"We didn't want to bother her," Cedric said quickly.

Then Opal added, "We didn't think she would believe us."

"No," Ruby said, "she certainly would not have believed you. But I'm glad you came here. I'll keep my third eye out for any signs of Swamy, but in the meantime,"—she addressed Opal directly then—"I believe you should proceed as if he's still alive." The woman's reaction was about what Ruby had suspected it would be. A certain flash of guilt lit up her eyes before it was gone as quickly as it had appeared.

She allowed them a few more sips of their tea before she stood and strongly hinted that it was time for them to be going. Thankfully, they took the hint.

"Do be safe," she said as they stepped out onto her porch. "Cedric, it would be best if you walked Opal all the way to her home."

"Of course."

As soon as she shut the door behind them, she turned to face Clifford where he'd been pretending to sleep by the fire. "There's much more to that story," she said.

"I couldn't agree more." He stood up and stretched his front legs, performing an elegant downward-facing hellhound. *"Are we following them, then?"*

Ruby grabbed her sweater from the hook by the door and slung it over her shoulders. "Of course we are."

Her familiar trotted over to her side. "I love a good late-night prowl."

Chapter Ten

Bloom checked the clock in her office. Ten fifteen in the morning. Ruby had asked to meet at ten o'clock, but she still wasn't there. It wasn't like her to be late. Over her thousands of years in existence, Bloom had noticed a peculiar phenomenon where people with very little to do in their daily lives managed to be late to everything. Perhaps time was simply less consequential to them, so why bother keeping track? But Ruby wasn't like that. She was the opposite. Perhaps it was her constant awareness of death that made the Fifth Wind more conscientious of the time.

"Should we be worried?" asked Zax Banderfield from where he sat in a solid oak chair across the desk from the sheriff.

"I'm honestly not sure," Bloom replied. "It's unusual behavior for her, but she can take care of herself. And she's smart enough to bring the hellhound with her when she does something extra foolish, so I usually don't worry about her."

But maybe she should start.

Zax shifted restlessly in his chair. "Maybe she forgot?"

"I don't see how she would. She only sent the message for us to meet last night."

"This morning, technically," he corrected. "I heard the owl bell ring outside my door at two fifteen this morning."

"Right, right."

Ruby's message hadn't been especially detailed. At least hers hadn't. (She couldn't speak to the one Zax had received.) It simply said, *Lead fell into my lap. Meet at your office at ten a.m. to discuss. RT*.

While it was always nice to receive confirmation that her hunch of a new lead surfacing was yet again proven accurate, Bloom would have been much happier if she knew Ruby was okay.

Because all too often, when a lead fell into one's lap, it wasn't a lead but rather a dangling carrot that led straight into a trap.

At twenty after the hour, Zax cleared his throat, causing Bloom to look up from the paperwork she was distractedly filling out.

"I think I'm going to return to Fluke Mountain," he said. "She must have forgotten about the meeting. I have quite a few things to do before the weekend arrives."

While Bloom wished he would hold out just a little longer, she couldn't blame him for wanting to get on with his day. Waiting twenty minutes was already generous for someone juggling the responsibilities he had.

"Very well."

Zax stood. "If you hear from Ruby, will you let me know?"

She didn't miss the lines of concern around his eyes. "Of course."

"Thank you, Sheriff. Good luck with..."—he gazed around the stacks—"all of this."

"If only luck had anything to do with it, I would have hired a full team of leprechauns by now. Take care of yourself up on the mountain, Mr. Banderfield."

He nodded and strode to the door, pulling it open and...

Ruby's fist pounded him in the sternum twice before she was able to catch herself. "Oh!" she said from the other side of the threshold. "I'm sorry. I thought you were the door." She massaged her knuckles. "Except the door is softer."

Zax stared down at her in mild amusement, but Bloom didn't miss the hint of relief as he shook his head.

It was the same emotion she felt upon seeing Ruby's small body draped in her usual black robes and baggy knitted sweater. Clifford hovered just a half step behind his witch.

"And I thought you would be here at ten," Zax said.

"Yes, that was the plan, but I was up terribly late, and managed to oversleep. Can't swing the late hours like I used to." She stepped around Zax and entered the office with Clifford. The werebear allowed them to pass and then shut the door again and returned to his seat.

While Gabby scooted two piles out of the way so she could have a clear view of Ruby's face, the Fifth Wind settled herself into the chair and stretched her neck. "I think I slept funny. Slept like the dead, as they say, although we all know those pests don't sleep. Anyway..."

Zax's eyes were glued to Ruby with a mixture of amusement and... something else. Bloom couldn't put her finger on it, but it carried a piercing intensity.

Ruby turned to address him, and his head jerked back a bit at the sudden attention. "Do you know," she said, "that two of your sleuth are involved in a sordid love affair?"

He blinked. "I don't know the specifics you're referring to, but werebears do tend to be amorous. Overly so."

Ruby shuddered, swallowed hard, then lifted her chin. "I'd say."

The sheriff cut in with, "And which werebears are we talking about here?"

"Opal Barker and Cedric Pine."

Bloom exchanged a quick glance with Zax, who seemed equally caught unaware by this. "I assume this has something to do with why you were up late last night."

"Indeed, Sheriff. In-deed. I had a knock on my door late last night and who should it be but those two. Now, I've never met Cedric before, but as you know, he looks strikingly like his brother, Virgil, so I was able to guess he was a Pine. Anywho, they came to see me because they swore they'd just gotten a glimpse of Taurus."

Bloom rolled her eyes. "Not that again."

"Oh yes. That. Again."

"When did they see him?" Zax said.

"Right after the restaurant at the lodge closed, after the last diners left. They were both finishing up their shifts, and apparently *very* busy in the kitchen when Opal claims to have seen the mythical creature staring at them through the window." She went on to recollect the rest of their story, and Bloom was glad to see no one else in the room appeared to believe much of the cock-and-bull story either.

"So, naturally," Ruby finished, "Cliff and I followed them."

Zax's brows furrowed. "You followed them in the dead of night when there was the possibility of a murderous minotaur running around?"

"I think you'll agree, knowing what you know now, and considering I already strongly suspected something was off with them, that they were and still are the prime suspects. I had to see what they were up to, especially when their story had so many temporal gaps in it."

Bloom nodded. She would have done the same. "What exactly did you find when you followed them?"

"I won't go into all the details, but Cedric did as I said and walked Opal all the way home. But he didn't stop on her doorstep. He followed her inside. And after a few minutes of silence, I decided it was best to see if I couldn't get a look indoors."

"Voyeur," Bloom muttered under her breath.

"Really!" Ruby snapped, trying to keep a straight face. "You think I wanted to see any of that? For all I knew, he'd followed her inside to attack her. Perhaps he was actually the one who had attacked his brother in the woods! It would make sense for Virgil to want to cover for his brother and make up some insane story about Taurus attacking him." She paused. "But in the end, he was not attacking her. Well, in a way he was mauling her, but she didn't seem to mind."

Zax's eyebrows raised, but he didn't seem especially abashed by the tale. Surprised, yes, but not embarrassed.

Bloom said, "I assume you didn't see anything resembling Taurus while you were on your night jaunt, did you?"

"Of course not," Ruby said. "That whole thing is made up, I'm convinced. Oh, don't look like that, Zax. You honestly can't believe in it, can you?"

The werebear shrugged. "I always thought it was a legend, but there's been an awful lot of talk about it lately, and now there are three sightings and a missing person. I don't know what to believe, so I'm keeping an open but skeptical mind."

Ruby frowned. "You didn't know about Opal and Cedric, did you?"

"I didn't have a clue. But you know how it goes working in restaurants."

Ruby cocked her head to the side. "I don't, actually."

"Yeah," Bloom added. "Neither do I. I only ever worked retail before I came here. Please enlighten us about how the service industry leads to cheating."

And now he did look slightly abashed, but he answered anyway. "Oh, just that, you know, you work in a high-pressure environment closely with others, and... well, stress and long hours, and shared experience... it can often lead to this kind of thing."

"So can a lack of loyalty in *any* scenario," Bloom snipped before she could stop herself.

Pull back, Gabby.

Her judgment often flared up like that when people

talked of disloyalty. Civilization was a hearty thing, all in all, but if one thing could threaten to unravel it, it was betrayal. And cheating was the most severe and devastating of all the betrayals. The hurt it caused sent shockwaves out into the universe.

But she reeled in her judgment and added, "Regardless, I agree with Ruby that Opal and Cedric are now our top suspects. Her live-in boyfriend is missing, and we discover she's been cheating with another man."

Zax said, "But how do we know this didn't start *after* Swamy went missing? It's been a few days. Maybe she's just in a state and Cedric capitalized on it? Gave her a little comfort."

Ruby shook her head firmly. "Again, I won't go into details, but I can tell you the way they were going at it made it clear this was *not* their first encounter."

Bloom cringed and held up a hand to stop to the discussion of it there. "I think the more likely scenario is that they've been carrying on in secret for a while. Perhaps Swamy confronted Cedric about it and things went too far. Maybe Cedric retaliated and ended up gravely injuring Swamy or worse. Or maybe Swamy simply discovered the infidelity and decided to move elsewhere."

"We could check at the train station," Ruby suggested. "See if the ticketmaster remembers him buying a ticket to Avalon."

Bloom nodded, but before she could follow that idea further, Zax interrupted.

"But what about Virgil?" he asked. "Where does his attack fit into this new theory?"

Bloom shrugged. "It could be completely unrelated, for all we know. Or perhaps he came upon Cedric and Swamy having it out and was injured when he involved himself in the dispute. It's not so much a theory as it is conjecture at this point. At least until we find something more substantial. However, I believe the relationship between Opal and Cedric is not insignificant. I agree that they're our best leads. We should go speak with them immediately." She paused, reaching to grab this morning's edition of the *Eastwind Watch* off the top of a pile of forms. Ruby wasn't the only one with an interesting development in the case this morning. "But first, we should probably address what the *Watch* published on the front page this morning." She held it out for Ruby to see. She and Zax had already discussed it while waiting for Ruby to arrive, and they seemed to be of the same mind on it.

As Ruby read the headline, her fiery brows pinched together, and as she went on to skim the rest of the article, the corners of her lips drooped further and further down into a deep frown.

She looked up at Bloom. "Typical drivel from Arthur Flufferbum. No legitimate sources named, mostly hearsay."

"Obviously," said Bloom. "But the point is that this so-called exposé on Taurus attacks is only going to fan the flames. I wouldn't be surprised if reports of sightings start pouring in from Fluke Mountain."

Zax jumped in. "The Sheriff and I have already made a plan for me to reach out to my sleuth and tell them the reports are false and that Flufferbum is just going for sensationalism."

Ruby tilted her head at him. "You think that will work?"

"It couldn't hurt. And besides, weres have been on the wrong end of sensational journalism since sensational journalism began. We're used to seeing lies between the lines."

"But isn't Flufferbum himself a were?" Ruby asked.

"Werebunny," Zax clarified. "So yes, but no. Witches tolerate werebunnies. Not much harm they can do in their shifted form."

"Tell that to my garden," Ruby said. "But point taken."

"The question is," Bloom said, trying to get the conversation back on track, "that someone involved in this has spoken to the *Watch* about it. So who was it, and what would they get out of it?"

"There's really only one way to find out," Ruby said. "Someone has to go speak with Arthur Flufferbum."

The women met eyes for only a split second.

"Not it," Bloom and Ruby both spat.

Then they turned to Zax. "I said it first," Ruby said. "You heard me say it first, right?"

Zax sputtered, clearly unsure of the best move here.

"You know I said it first," Bloom added. "I was clearly the first to say it."

Again, Zax opened his mouth, but nothing decipherable came out.

"Fine," Bloom said. "You win, Ruby. You and Zax can go interview Opal and Cedric, and I'll speak with that Flufferbum fool." She stood from her chair, glad for an excuse to get out of the office and take decisive action of one kind or another, even if it meant entering the offices of the *Eastwind Watch*, a newspaper with a long legacy of printing incorrect information bordering on libel regarding the Eastwind Sheriff's Department.

But no sooner had she adjusted her stiff wings than she felt the summons from Deputy Titterfield.

Heaven's hearth! This better be good...

She paused, considering her priorities. She couldn't be everywhere at once, unfortunately.

The choice was obvious. Her brother in uniform came first when she was on the clock (and if that also gave her an excuse to put off her interview with Flufferbum, she wouldn't cry about it). She'd blessed the deputy with that summoning spell for a reason, and he hadn't abused it yet.

She turned to address Ruby and Zax, who were standing now as well. "I apologize. I just got summoned by Deputy Titterfield, and I would be failing in my duty if I ignored it. You two go ahead and speak with Opal and Cedric. Once I handle this professional matter, I'll speak with Arthur and then meet up with you when I can."

Neither Zax nor Ruby raised an objection to the plan. Big surprise.

Because she'd given them the perfect official excuse to spend a little alone time with each other, and neither was fool enough to pass that up.

Chapter Eleven

Ruby walked with Zax on her left and Clifford on her right as they made their way up the mountain toward Treetop Lodge.

Breathe through the nose, Ruby reminded herself over and over again. There was no reason for her to be in shape, but that didn't mean she wanted to make it clear to Zax that she was out of shape. And focusing on her breathing allowed him to do most of the talking on their walk, which she didn't mind.

Unfortunately, he was focused solely on the case, rolling through the facts, mulling over conjectures. When he finally paused for a moment, she asked on a quick exhale, "How does someone become head of the werebears?"

He seemed to like that question, but most everyone she'd ever met liked talking about themselves, so it was her time-tested strategy for derailing a conversation. "It involves a solid reputation and good fighting skills," he said. "When Montel Fontaine stepped down, I was only twenty and foolish enough to think I could take on any bear in the sleuth in claw-to-claw combat."

"Foolish? But didn't you win?"

"Well, yes, but it was through sheer luck. I was an idiot to think it could have happened any other way. I was up against Linton Stormstruck in the final match, and he stepped in a small hole at just the right moment. Well, the wrong moment for him, but the right one for me. He stumbled, and I leapt on him and managed to pin him with claws pressing against the skin of his throat." He looked down at Ruby. "We don't fight to the death. We're *somewhat* civilized." He returned his gaze to the ascending path. "Anyway, that's how I became the leader. Well, that, plus the rest of the bears approved my leadership. But that always happens for the combat victor. The vote is just a formality." He paused. "I wouldn't be leader if it weren't for a little bit of luck. I never let myself forget that. Linton was a fierce fighter, and he would have beaten me ninety-nine times out of one hundred. All the Stormstrucks are fierce fighters."

"Swamy included?" Ruby asked.

"From what I've seen, yes. Which is why I'm almost ready to believe that Taurus is running around in the Silent Reach. Only something that fierce could have overpowered a bear like Swamy without leaving a trace. Perhaps a lesser being could have snuck up on Swamy and dealt a quick death blow, but for there to be no blood or trace of death means that Swamy would have still been alive when he was taken. And I can't imagine him not putting up a fight if he remained at all conscious."

"That *is* a disturbing prospect," Ruby replied. "I understand you were involved in the search party yesterday?"

"Sure was. Deputy Titterfield put me in charge of organizing the search in the middle third of the Reach. We combed all the way to the creek. One of the volunteers was a werewolf, and his nose picked up a scent of Swamy, but we lost it at the creek. Didn't pick it up again anywhere within our perimeter."

She allowed herself a moment to puzzle over the new information, then asked, "How deep is the creek?"

"Doesn't get more than five feet deep in the middle."

"Could he have drowned in that shallow of water? Then perhaps his body floated down the river?"

Zax shrugged. "I don't see how that's impossible. But he was well over six feet tall. Seems strange that he would drown where his feet could touch the bottom with his head completely out of water."

Yes, that did seem strange. "Perhaps someone helped him along. Then it's just a matter of guiding the body along with the current. The creek leads where?"

"Widow Lake."

Ruby frowned. It was what she'd expected, but that didn't make it good news. "If his body is in Widow Lake, we'll never find it. I doubt anyone would want to try." There were things in that lake that people whispered about. And worse, there were things in that lake no one even dared whisper about. There was a reason the town's only vampire had settled there and built himself a castle on a small peninsula jutting out into the water. Only fools would darken his doorstep.

"You think he's dead, though?" Zax asked.

"I don't know. He hasn't paid me a home visit, if that's what you mean. And if someone snuck up on him and drowned him, I'd be surprised if his spirit simply accepted that and moved on. It's a perfect recipe for a restless spirit."

The lodge came into view, and Ruby was grateful for that. All the chatter on top of the climb had asked far too much of her lungs.

Ruby had overheard Opal and Cedric mention working the following day when she'd followed them back to Opal's home the night before.

But when the host greeted Ruby, Zax, and Clifford and Zax asked to speak with the pair, the host simply shook his overgrown mane of blond hair and said, "They ain't here today."

"Who is?" Zax asked.

"Virgil Pine and Abigail Shoggins, sir."

Ruby met Zax's eyes, and he seemed to be thinking the same thing as she was: the suspects had fled.

Zax said, "We'd like to speak with Virgil, then, if you don't mind."

The young host nodded and went to fetch him.

"Where do you think they are?" Ruby asked.

"Who knows. If they're the ones behind Swamy's disappearance, I'd guess they hopped the first train to Avalon today. They may already be deep in the woods of Wisconsin by now."

"That would be the smart thing to do if they wanted to evade justice, yes, but do they strike you as especially intelligent?"

The werebear considered it. "Not especially. But fleeing is something even a dumb criminal would do. They just wouldn't do it particularly well."

"And that's assuming they're the criminals," she added, "but what if they're not? Then how could we explain this behavior?"

Before he could reply, Virgil stomped out of the kitchen looking frazzled and stopped in his tracks when his eyes landed on Ruby. He rolled his shoulders back and approached at a less hurried rate.

"Morning, Sleuth Leader. Morning, Ruby."

"Morning," Ruby replied, and Zax simply said, "A word outside?"

Virgil glanced over his shoulder at the two tables with occupants and hesitated. "It's just me and Abigail right now."

"Abigail," Zax called to her as she was carrying an empty tray to the kitchen. She looked up, saw who it was, and her eyes grew large. "We need to steal Virgil for a second. Would you cover for him?"

She nodded adamantly, and Zax nodded and rewarded her with a charming grin.

"There," he said, turning to Virgil, "you're all set."

But Virgil's hesitance didn't end there. He slinked after Zax as they exited the restaurant, cut through the lobby of the lodge, and stepped out into the pleasant spring air.

"I understand you weren't scheduled to work today," said Zax, jumping right into it. Ruby appreciated the candor.

Virgil nodded. "Yeah, my brother sent me a message

asking if I'd cover for him today. He said he wasn't feeling well."

"And was Abigail scheduled to work?"

Virgil shrugged. "How would I know?"

Ruby arched an eyebrow at him. "Is there not a schedule posted?"

"Well, sure, but why bother checking it? I just come in when I'm told and leave when I'm cut."

Ruby doubted that, but she let it drop. The fact that he was being this evasive meant he knew something was up, and had known since before they'd arrived, most likely.

"So you don't know where Opal is right now?" Zax asked.

"Nope. She isn't my responsibility... thankfully."

Ruby cocked her head to the side. "And what do you mean by that?"

"Nothing," he said quickly. "She's just one of those women who's a handful."

"I'm not sure what you mean," Ruby persisted, feeling slightly offended on Opal's behalf and wondering vaguely how many men had referred to *her* as "a handful" in that diminishing tone before.

He looked like he was about to clam up completely, but Zax stepped in. "You mean she gets around?"

Ruby stifled a gasp at the bluntness, then felt a warm heat in her chest as she stared at Zax's confident expression.

Virgil shifted his weight on his feet then finally said, "Yeah, that's about it."

"Has she been unfaithful to Swamy with anyone besides your brother?"

"You know about that?"

"I could ask you the same," Zax countered.

Virgil paused, a muscle in his jaw flexing. Then he said, "Nah, no one that I know of. I mean, it's not that she hasn't tried."

Both Zax and Ruby stayed quiet, and Virgil went on. "She came onto me a few months back, okay? We were working late together, and—please don't mention this to Cedric."

"Of course not," said Zax and Ruby together.

"After our shift, we were closing up, wiping down tables and such, and... she cornered me. Right there in the dining room! Windows all around, a straight view from the lodge. Anyone could have seen." He paused. "And, you know... I think someone did."

Ruby's gut clenched and she already guessed what he was about to say, but she needed to hear it anyway. "Who was that?"

Virgil couldn't meet their eyes, but instead stared at the ground and kicked at some of the decomposing pine needles instead. "Swamy. I think he mighta seen."

Zax leaned in close. "Seen what?"

"She kissed me. And, unfortunately, I didn't have a good mind to push her off me right away. I mean, it's Opal. She's not exactly ugly, and she's always been a good time to work with. But then I remembered she was in a relationship, and I broke the kiss."

"And you saw Swamy watching?" Zax asked.

"Well, no. But he appeared in the lobby to walk her home maybe twenty seconds later. And he was acting a little strange."

"What do you mean?" Ruby prodded.

Virgil squinted up toward the treetops now, his face scrunching with strain. "I don't know. Maybe a little too friendly? I might have just been paranoid. Maybe I was expecting him to rush in and kick my hide for kissing his woman, and when he didn't... it all seemed off. But then again, maybe he just didn't see it. Maybe I got lucky with timing for once."

Zax said, "And you said this was a couple of months ago?"

"Yeah."

"Is that why you waited to mention it?"

"Huh?" Virgil met his eyes now, and genuine concern filled them. "No, no. I didn't wait to tell you like I was holding it back. I just thought of it now. I mean, fang and claws, Zax, if you haven't heard the rumors about her before, you haven't been paying attention! I only told you my story because I know it as a fact. But I've heard tales from plenty of other werebears about them having similar experiences with her... and some of them didn't claim to have exercised the restraint I did."

"I'm glad to see you can separate fact from conjecture," Zax said sharply. "Because we do not spread rumors about each other in this sleuth, understand?"

Virgil held his hands up, palms out. "Oh, trust me, I know! Why do you think I mentioned my situation first? Like I said, everything else is just rumor, and I wouldn't have mentioned it to anyone but the two of you and for this situation."

Ruby cut in. "You think her cheating is relevant to this situation?"

He shrugged. "Could be. But then again, it might just be a matter of Taurus."

Ruby shut her eyes so no one could see her roll them.

"You stick by that?" Zax said. "That it was Taurus who attacked you in the woods?"

"I do," Virgil replied firmly. "I'll admit, I started doubting my own eyes right after I spoke with you both the first time, but then... I saw him again last night."

Chapter Twelve

Ruby's eyes shot wide. "You did? You saw Taurus last night?"

She turned to Zax to get his reaction, but he was unreadable as he stared at Virgil.

"Yeah. And I know you don't believe me. But trust me when I say I'd rather it be anything else that I've seen twice now. I don't *want* it to be Taurus, but there's just no getting around it, as far as I'm concerned. He's attacked me once"—he clutched the bandage on his arm—"and if I hadn't hurried inside last night, I think he might've attacked me again."

"And where were you when this occurred?" Zax said.

"At home. I was sitting on the front porch, having a drink and whittling a rattle for the Fontaines' new baby girl. I heard a rustling in the woods and near about wet myself when I saw something large move between two trees. I'm not embarrassed to tell you I hurried my hide inside the house and locked the door, and when I looked out the window, I saw him. He'd come out of the clearing and was heading straight for my cabin."

"And then what?"

Virgil cringed. "I don't know. I hurried to the closet under the stairs to grab the battle hammer my grandfather passed down to me, and then spent the rest of the night in my bedroom clutching the thing."

While Virgil wasn't as tall as Cedric or Zax, he was by no means a dainty man, and the fact that someone of his stature would be so afraid of whatever it was that was outside his window shook Ruby more than she liked to admit. It took everything in her not to check over her shoulder at that very minute to make sure nothing was creeping out of the woods that surrounded the lodge. Thankfully, she had Clifford by her side, and he could smell a threat a hundred yards downwind of him.

"Describe to me again," she said, "what Taurus looked like?"

Virgil humored her, and the description hadn't changed since the first time.

"See, here's the thing," she said. "I've researched Taurus since we last met, and what slim information there is says nothing about him being anything other than a purebred minotaur. But what you describe seems to be more of a cross between a minotaur and a werebear."

"Maybe the legend got it wrong," Virgil offered.

"Hmm..." said Ruby, unconvinced. "Would you help me disprove a theory, Mr. Pine?"

He straightened up and nodded.

"Would you remove your bandages for a moment?"

The werebears swapped confused looks, then Virgil shrugged and agreed.

Once the bandages were removed, Ruby inspected the wounds on his arm.

They were deep and angry, that was for sure, and the entire area was covered in tar-like remnants of a clotted, muddy substance. "Is this the salve you made?" she asked Zax.

"Yes."

"And does it contain any phoenix blood?"

His cocoa eyebrows shot up his forehead. "No. Why?"

Rather than answering, she turned to Virgil. "Has the skin begun to rot at all? Any sort of yellowing around the edges of the wound? Any peeling?"

Virgil cringed at the description. "No. Not at all. Why?"

She leaned closer over the wounds, inspecting them until she was satisfied. Then she stepped back and said, "Minotaur wounds are necrotic. They kill the skin and tissue, rot it away. The only way to stop that process from happening is with a salve that includes phoenix blood. Therefore, I can conclude with some degree of certainty that you were not attacked by a minotaur."

Virgil blinked at her. "Okay. But that doesn't mean it wasn't Taurus. Maybe his claws don't work the same."

Ruby was losing her patience with this nonsense, but she knew it wouldn't help her achieve her goal if she let it show. "You mentioned that people had been bringing up Taurus a lot prior to your alleged encounter with him."

Virgil nodded.

"Was there anyone who talked about it more than others?" It was her Insight that had led her to ask this question, and it was her Insight that guessed the answer before he spoke it.

"Well, yes. But... I promised I wouldn't say anything."

"Ooh, this is interesting," Clifford said.

Zax took the bait. "Wouldn't say anything about what?"

"He didn't want me to tell anyone because he was afraid no one would believe him. And now that I've seen it too and told people, I know he was right." A bitterness crept into Virgil's rushed words. "I mean, heck, I didn't really believe him when he said it. If I had, I wouldn't have gone."

Zax took a hurried step closer to Virgil and barked, "Slow down." He did. "Who didn't want you to tell anyone that he'd seen Taurus?"

"Swamy."

"And where wouldn't you have gone?"

"The Silent Reach. That's where he'd seen Taurus. He said he'd seen the thing a couple of times, and one had been the night before in the Silent Reach. He asked if I wanted to go for a run with him to track it, and I agreed."

"And that was the night you were attacked in the woods?" Ruby asked.

Virgil balled his hands into fists and shoved them in the pockets of his apron. "Yeah."

Ruby found this new development equal parts interesting and infuriating, and Zax seemed to be on the same page. His impatience was poorly disguised as he asked his next question. "How come you never mentioned that you had plans to meet with Swamy the night you were attacked and the night before he went missing?"

Virgil opened his mouth to respond, but nothing came out. His eyes bounced between Ruby and Zax, and eventually landed on his leader. "Well, it would have seemed suspicious, wouldn't it? I make plans with the missing person, and I come back with scratches on me. Might look like I tried to kill him but failed, so I finished the job the next night."

"Yes," Ruby said softly, "it might look just like that."

"But I didn't!" he protested. "That wasn't how it went down at all! So I didn't see why mentioning it would have done anyone any good. Besides, I never even saw him that night."

Ruby's breath caught in her chest. "Which night? The night you two were going into the Silent Reach or the night he disappeared?"

"The first one. Well, both, actually. We were supposed to meet there after I got off my shift and closed up. At eleven o'clock, we said. I got off work early, though, and decided to head straight out."

"And what time was that?" Ruby prodded.

"Maybe ten forty-five or thereabouts. Not too much earlier."

"And how long were you out there before the attack happened?"

"Maybe five minutes? I'd just had enough time to shift and get a few runs in. That's when I saw him."

"Swamy?" she asked.

"No, Taurus. He was standing on the other side of the creek from me."

Ruby's vision of Taurus charging flashed back into her mind and sent a wave of goosebumps washing over her skin. "And you never saw Swamy in the Reach that night?"

"No. As soon as I was attacked, I fled back home. I spent the rest of the night shook up and cleaning my wounds. I wasn't sure what to do because I knew no one would believe me. By the next night, the scratches were looking so bad that I asked Zax if he'd bring something over in the morning. "

"Did you contact Swamy to let him know what happened?"

"I did. I thought about going over to his house, but, well, I was scared to leave mine. So I sent an owl over, asking him to come see me after work the next day so we could talk."

"And did he?"

"No. He never responded and never showed."

By that point, Virgil was appearing entirely browbeaten, his eyes downcast and his shoulders hunched, and Ruby suspected there wasn't much left to wring out of him. It was unfortunate that he'd not mentioned all of this sooner, but she understood his reasoning. The whole situation didn't look good for him.

"We'd better let you get back to work," she said, and Virgil nodded somberly.

Zax, meanwhile, had stood silently with his thick arms crossed in front of his broad chest for the entire last part of the conversation, and remained that way as Virgil turned and left.

Was he too disappointed in his sleuth member's conduct to speak, or was that suspicion on his face?

Ruby waited until Virgil was back inside, then said, "Care for a cup of tea?"

Chapter Thirteen

Bloom was thankful to be done with the ruckus down at Sheehan's Pub (five leprechauns, two werewolves, and a knife-wielding pixie in custody until they could all cool down and make good with each other), but she cringed at the thought of how much paperwork was going to come out of it.

Deputy Titterfield had been right to summon her when he did; the pixie had a crazed look in his eyes, and three of the leprechauns had stuck themselves to a shouting and flailing werewolf by the time she'd arrived.

Brawls down at Sheehan's weren't uncommon, even before noon on a Friday, but they could get ugly.

However, now she had another important task to attend to and expected it to make prying leprechauns off a werewolf seem like a fun party game in comparison.

The exterior of the *Eastwind Watch*'s headquarters was as self-reverential as anyone who'd read the newspaper might expect. It was a wide, one-story stone building with the words *The Eastwind Watch* carved into an ornate stone archway above the entrance. And below that inscription was, in bold Enochian letters, their motto, which they told everyone translated to "A clear eye in uncertain times."

Of course, as one of the only three beings in Eastwind who knew Enochian, the language of angels, and as the only fluent speaker, Sheriff Bloom knew that the phrase translated to more precisely to, "A transparent eyeball in probable intervals."

She'd never bothered to correct them on it, mostly because it gave her a much needed chuckle every time she saw it printed at the top of the daily paper. And seeing it carved in stone for generations to come was even more delightful.

On each side of the archway was a statue—the one on the left was a witch pointing his wand up toward Heaven (or the general direction of it), and on the right was a werewolf, mid-shift, howling (again, in the general direction of Heaven).

How pretentious can you get? she thought.

Bloom passed between the statues and under the archway and entered through the heavy wooden doors.

As stately as the outside looked, the inside was an entirely different story.

While a prim and proper elf sat patiently behind a stone reception desk and asked the sheriff how she could help her, just a little farther on inside, a faun sprinted from one cubical to another, screaming incoherently with a fistful of parchment in his hand, and two ogres shouted monosyllabically at one another across a flimsy wooden desk. Owls swooped low overhead, grabbing sheets of parchment from raised hands and dropping them on the heads of other employees who hardly seemed to notice. Bloom thought she smelled smoke, but she decided not to inquire further into that; unless she saw flames, there was no need to make it her problem.

"Can I help you?" the elf asked again, smiling like nothing insane was happening right behind her.

"I need to speak with Mr. Flufferbum."

The elf's grin grew wider, but it didn't quite show her teeth. "I'm afraid he's terribly busy at the moment."

"I assume he's always busy, if not with the publication, with keeping this place from collapsing in on itself. But I need to speak with him anyway. It's official sheriff's business. And it's urgent."

The elf's practiced smile drooped. "Fine. Stay here." And then she turned on her heel and stomped off. Before she disappeared around the corner, an owl came too near to her head, and she swatted it away. It squawked angrily at her before carrying on with its business.

A few minutes later, the elf returned, looking much worse for the wear, and escorted Bloom past the chaos of the cubicles and into a private office.

Arthur Flufferbum didn't look up from the papers on his desk, even as the elf announced Bloom's presence and left the two of them alone, shutting the door just a little harder than necessary on her way out.

The werebunny was stooped over a long sheet of parchment, a looking glass pressed against his eye as he inspected the document. Teetering at the front edge of his desk, having been carelessly knocked around by the chaos of papers surrounding it, was a placard that read *Arthur Q. Flufferbum, Chief Editor.*

She couldn't judge the state of his desk, considering

the perpetual state of hers, but she *could* judge his rudeness in ignoring her. And so she did.

"I need only a minute of your time, Mr. Flufferbum."

He scribbled out a line of text and, without looking up, said, "Get on with it then."

"You published information about the attacks yesterday and cited an anonymous source. I need to know who gave you that information."

He scoffed as he straightened his spine, but at least he finally looked up and met her eye. "Do I need to define 'anonymous' for you?"

For Heaven's sake. "You're saying you don't know who supplied the information?"

"Again, do I need to define 'anonymous' for you?"

She could have gotten mad at him. She could have done that very easily. But that wasn't how you played against someone like Flufferbum. He *wanted* to make her mad; there might be a story in it.

She wouldn't give him that.

"How do you know the source isn't lying if you don't know who it is?"

"Why would they lie?"

"The same reason anyone lies."

"Which is?"

"It varies. But usually people lie because it benefits them."

He rolled his beady eyes. "We don't issue payments to anonymous sources."

"As you know full well, there are other ways to benefit from events that might strike fear into the heart of the public. And I'd say an article about Taurus in the Silent Reach might do just that."

Flufferbum said nothing, simply shrugged like it wasn't his problem.

"Fine," Bloom asked. "You don't have to tell me anything you may or may not know, but can I at least see the primary document for myself?"

Flufferbum wiggled his bristly mustache but didn't break eye contact. "No."

"Why not?"

"Two reasons. First, you want to get a sample of the handwriting and try to match it to the sender. And second, I burned the correspondence myself. It's standard procedure."

She arched an eyebrow at him and crossed her arms over her chest. "Destroying evidence is standard procedure?"

"You sure see things in black and white, Sheriff. No, we're not destroying evidence, we're ensuring the public doesn't lose trust in our ability to protect their anonymity if they so choose to use it. We're protecting them from this very scenario, where the overzealous law comes marching in, trying to claim jurisdiction over the press."

"For fang's sake," she said, letting the expletive slip and hoping immediately that it wouldn't make the next day's edition. "I'm not doing anything of the sort. We have a missing person case on our hands. I'm just trying to find him before it's too late, if it isn't already."

"Justify it however you like. It amounts to the same thing."

He had a lot of nerve to accuse her of spinning the situation, but she decided not to say that. Instead, she strode to the edge of his desk, staring down at him where he sat. His mustache began to twitch furiously, but he clenched his jaw and continued to meet her gaze.

"If we discover Swamy Stormstruck's body," she said, "and I find out there was anything you could have done to help us prevent his death, I hope you understand that I will not hesitate to arrest you for interfering in a law enforcement investigation. You're not a doctor or a lawyer, you're not required to keep confidentiality. You're choosing to do so, and that makes you entirely responsible for that choice."

"I wish you would just—"

"Do you understand me?"

"I don't think—"

"Do you understand me?"

He jolted back, his beady eyes blinking rapidly as his nostrils flared almost imperceptibly. "Perfectly."

"Good." She found that she was leaning sharply over the desk, and she cleared her throat and inhaled deeply to steady herself.

But then something on the parchment he'd been inspecting caught her eye. She was sure she'd just seen the name Opal written there.

With lightning speed, she snatched the paper before he could stop her and hurried back a few steps to give herself space to read over it.

"What do you think you're doing?" he demanded.

But she didn't listen. He'd have to come over and rip this paper from her grip if he wanted her to stop what she was doing.

And that was exactly what he did.

He hurried around his desk and rushed toward her.

Thank goddess for her speed reading. By the time he reached her, she handed it back to him without a fight.

"What is that drivel? Surely you're not running it."

He stuck out his chin defiantly. "It's front page on tomorrow's edition, yes."

"You can't publish that."

"I absolutely can."

"Fine, you can. But you'll be hearing about it."

He chuckled dryly. "From whom?"

The name rolled right off her tongue without a single thought. "Zax Banderfield." It seemed to cause the werebunny pause, so she continued in the same vein. "And Count Sebastian Malavic." That really did the trick. The *Eastwind Watch* liked to boast about being independent and uninfluenced, but it accepted quite a lot of funding from the town's purse. And that line item was ultimately signed off on by the treasurer of the High Council.

And the treasurer of the High Council was none other than the town's only vampire, the wealthy Count Sebastian Malavic, whose reputation preceded him in an icy chill.

"I'm going to run it," Arthur said, though the shake in his voice was unmistakable. "The decision's already been made."

"Fine," Bloom said, enjoying the upper hand for once. "But you'd better tell me everything that's going to be in it. Everything."

And to her pleasure, Arthur Flufferbum grunted, spat "fine!", and then spilled the scoop.

Chapter Fourteen

✿✿✿

Zax didn't have any tea in his home on Fluke Mountain, but he had coffee. She accepted his offering hesitantly and made sure not to suck down the cup too quickly, lest her resulting bluntness get her in trouble.

Her stomach rumbled and reminded her that she'd left her home in such a hurry this morning that she'd forgotten to eat.

"Same," said Clifford.

Zax's home was so lavishly furnished, she wondered if he was married and simply hadn't mentioned it.

"Did you design this space yourself?" she asked once the two of them were seated at a table made from the cross section of an ancient tree. It looked like he'd made this himself, adding some sort of finish to bring out the gorgeous details of the tree's many circles. She rubbed her hand over the tabletop as he responded.

"I did. It took years, but I finally got it how I liked it. This"—he nodded down at the table—"was made from an oak on the other side of Fluke Mountain. Don't worry, it was already gone when I took this from it. I would never murder a beauty like that just for a nice table. But I wanted to preserve something of her once she was gone."

Ruby grinned at his fond use of the female pronoun. "I think that makes you a hero among the druids."

And now he grinned. "It did. And I made similar tables for a lot of them. I even made one for The High Priest Clearbrook."

"I suppose you think that will impress me, so I can tell you that I'm not his biggest fan."

"That's a relief. Because I made his out of the deadest part of the tree. He didn't know the difference. I sold it to him at a mark-up and told him it was actually a better cut than all the rest."

Ruby guffawed. "I'll take your secret to the grave."

"If you want. But part of me wants to him find out. I'd love to see what he'd do. Turn the Coven against me? Good luck. Not even a Coven witch would be dumb enough to go after the sleuth leader. They'd have a whole heap of werebears crashing down on them."

"It sounds from your tone that you might like that idea." She was fond of it as well, after her many unfavorable encounters with the Coven. But she wouldn't tell him that.

"Let's just say I don't *dislike* the idea. Especially after a High Council meeting. Mayor Periwinkle is insufferable. And I generally like North Winds!"

"Then we agree on that. They're usually the most practical."

"Petrov Periwinkle is just the most heartless. You should hear him when it comes time for budget discussions. He would cut the entire city's budget outside of his own paycheck if he could."

Ruby shook her head, and the conversation fell into a lull. She sipped her coffee cautiously. It was delicious, but she credited most of that to the bit of honeycomb he had put into each of their mugs. She noted the small luxury. It might just be her new favorite way to take her coffee.

She felt her stomach rumble again. Perhaps she could grab a bite at A New Leaf on her way back in town. A lemon poppyseed muffin sounded divine. And Clifford was especially fond of their little meat pies. He usually gobbled up five before he was satisfied.

"You know how Virgil said Swamy never showed?" Zax began once the friendly mood had settled.

Ruby nodded.

"Do we actually know who was the last person to see Swamy?"

Ruby considered it and was shocked to realize she hadn't sooner. Not closely, at least. "My presumption was that it was Opal who had seen him last. Or, if he's dead, whoever killed him."

"But we don't know that for sure," he said.

"No, I don't suppose we do. Are you saying what I think you're saying?"

"Depends. What do you think I'm saying?"

"That Swamy could have been missing for longer than we thought. That he could have actually gone missing in the woods the same night that Virgil was attacked."

"It could be," said Zax. "But not even Virgil saw him that night, or so he says. What if Swamy went missing even sooner? We don't have a clear idea of the last time he was seen."

Ruby nodded. As more facts surfaced and more interviews were conducted, reevaluating what she knew was becoming a full-time job. And one for which she likely wouldn't receive proper compensation. Ah, well, it wasn't like she was hurting for money. There was serious job security in dealing with restless spirits.

"Do we know where Swamy works?" she asked.

"You might not, but I do. He's one of the main growers for Whirligig's Garden Center."

"What does that mean?"

"He grows stuff."

"I know that," she snapped. "I meant more 'how does that job proceed?' Does he see Thaddeus Whirligig every day? Does he work alongside anyone else? Who, in other words, does he see regularly?"

"I believe he works in the woods. He plants the seeds for the trees and ferns and grows them to whatever size Whirligig orders."

"And he does this operation on his own?"

"As far as I know."

Ruby thought more on that. Alone in the woods day after day. Plenty of time to think. But also, plenty of time for something to go terribly wrong. "How close is his nursery to the Silent Reach?"

"From what I understand, it's nowhere near it. Whenever I pass him in the morning, I see him heading the opposite direction from his cabin."

"But you don't know exactly where it is?"

"No."

"For fang's sake," she muttered. "Then we'll have to

go on assuming he's not dead in the woods, though if he died of injury and it was a slow one, there's a good chance his spirit would simply move on and I wouldn't hear a peep from him." She sighed. "Everyone talks about how quick deaths are merciful, but the slow ones can allow a person to assemble their necessary peace before the end so they move straight on without lingering. And that's merciful to me." She took a deep sip of coffee, knowing even as she did it that she should slow down. But it was just too delicious.

"I think we need to pay Ms. Barker another visit," she said.

Zax nodded. "Exactly what I was thinking. But first, how about I fix us something to eat?"

She smiled. "You read my mind."

"I'm afraid I don't have much. Just salted meats and cheeses. I could make a platter."

Clifford wagged his tail and Ruby's empty stomach gave no complaint. "If you're as superb a detective as you are a host, Mr. Banderfield, I'll consider this case as good as solved."

Chapter Fifteen

While finishing the meats and cheeses, Ruby wrote out a quick message and sent it off to Bloom to let her know they were revisiting one of the prime suspects. It was smart to keep the sheriff apprised of their plans in case things went south, and though Ruby was traveling with a hellhound and a werebear who was easily twice her mass, she knew that size didn't always matter in the face of evil.

Was Opal evil? Had she killed her boyfriend?

The motive was shaky at best. Why kill him when she already had what she wanted: Cedric. However, the odds that she was covering for the real killer—a jealous lover, say—were quite high.

The afternoon was getting on when Ruby and Zax left his house.

She asked, "You really think she'll be at home?"

"It's worth a try. We already know she isn't at work."

"Perhaps she really is sick," Ruby mused.

After a moment, they both dismissed it. Even Clifford said that it was unlikely.

The cabin came into view, and Ruby considered a strategy. After all, not only were they entering into the home of a suspect, they were also entering into the home of the missing person. Having a solid approach in mind prior to entry was always smart. And if that approach involved a quick exit plan, even better.

"Keep watch?" Ruby said to Clifford when they were no more than fifteen feet from the front door.

The hellhound bowed his head. "*On it.*"

Zax observed her familiar with approval. "I could use one of those."

"I think you're intimidating enough as it is. If you start walking around with that kind of backup, everyone will think you're hiding a body or ten."

"Fair enough."

Ruby was just about to question whether the front door would be unlocked, considering the circumstances, when Zax twisted the handle and the door swung open.

Neither of them took a step inside right away. They simply stared in shock.

"Are you seeing what I'm seeing?" Ruby finally asked.

"A ransacked house?"

"They didn't live like this normally, did they?"

"I sure as swirls hope not."

Zax was the first to step forward into the mess. It looked like a tornado had touched down. In the living room, two of the three chairs lay on their side and the drawers of a wooden credenza had been forced open roughly. Two of the drawers were pulled all the way out, and the contents were strewn around the area.

And it didn't get better the further they walked into the residence.

"Opal?" Zax called. "Opal? Are you home?"

There was no reply, and with the alertness only a predator can summon, he slowly stalked deeper into the mess. "Are you okay? Do you need help?" He turned the corner into a hallway where three doors led off—two on the right, one on the left. Every door was open except the farthest on the right.

Ruby unabashedly used the werebear's large frame as a shield, and stayed as close to him as she could without stepping on his heels. She could fight if she had to—she'd done it before—but Fifth Wind powers weren't always the easiest to tap into, and it was never pretty when she had to do that. Lots of ghosts involved, spiritual residue everywhere. Messy stuff.

She had a wand, sure, but she hardly used it and almost never had it with her. Carrying around a handcrafted stick with overpriced labradorite in it was a great way to end up cracking that handcrafted stick with overpriced labradorite in two. (Granted, Ezra had given her a steep discount on it the first time around, but that was years ago. She doubted he would be so generous now.)

And besides, even basic magic that an East Wind or a South Wind could perform effortlessly cost her a great amount of energy. Lately, she'd had an easier time yanking a spirit into the corporal world kicking and screaming than she'd had using her wand to tidy her home. That was fine, though; she enjoyed the act of cleaning up. It was essentially what she did all the time: cleaning up messes.

But the mess in Opal's house was one she didn't think she would enjoy sorting out. Goddess help whoever ended up in charge of that. Hiring one of the expensive witch cleaning services would be worth it, and it took a lot for Ruby to admit that.

The first doorways on the left and right of the hall showed similar views of disarray, but no sign of Opal. Zax approached the closed door then. He hesitated before knocking. Then he knocked three times.

Ruby hurriedly added a fourth and glared at him, hissing, "What are you trying to do? Summon a demon?"

He recoiled slightly, staring at her in befuddlement. "Of course not."

Right. Of course not. Werebears didn't have to worry about things like that. "Never mind," she said, "I don't hear anything in there."

Zax turned the handle and opened the door slowly as Ruby held her breath.

It creaked on its hinges, sending goosebumps bolting down her spine. He peeked his head in, then suddenly exhaled and casually flung it open the rest of the way. "Nothing," he said, stepping to the side. The room looked exactly like the rest of the house. Whoever had done this had simply closed one door and not bothered with the rest.

Ruby felt a little silly about her anxiety, but gave herself a break. "Nobody home then?"

"Doesn't look like it," Zax replied, poking through a pile of clothes with the toe of his boot as if there might be something important hidden beneath.

Ruby ran her palms down the front of her robes.

"Very well then. I guess we have a pretty good idea of where Opal is now."

Zax caught her eye. "Dead and buried?"

"What? No! No, no, no. Well, I suppose it's possible, but I was imagining she'd be at Cedric Pine's home."

"Oh, yeah. That makes more sense."

"Then we shall head that way."

"What about all this mess?"

Ruby scanned it. "All I see is a bunch of piles of not-our-problem. Come on. Let's go catch those two love birds in their nest."

Chapter Sixteen

"Just up here," Zax said as he led Ruby and Clifford down the path on the way to their next interview. "That's where the Pines live." He pointed at a wide cabin with two small footpaths leading up to the front porch.

"The Pines? How many live there?"

"Just Cedric and Virgil."

Ruby inhaled so suddenly, she nearly choked. "Cedric and Virgil share a home?"

"No, no. The cabin is two connected homes. They live separately."

"This changes things," Clifford added.

"It certainly does. I'd assume the entire building was Cedric's home. But what, exactly does it change?"

"That's the question of the hour, I'd venture."

Something tugged at the back of her mind, some event that could make much more sense given this new context, but she would need a moment alone before she could dive deep enough to locate it and allow it the space it needed to breathe and grow into a tangible hunch.

As they drew closer, she did notice that the front porch was actually split in two by a small wooden divider in the middle. Well, it was no wonder Virgil knew about his brother's affair. The cabin's walls couldn't be that thick.

Cedric answered the door looking perfectly healthy, contrary to what he'd told his work. "Sleuth leader," he said, clearly not expecting the visit. "What can I do for you?"

Zax slapped on his most congenial smile and said, "I heard you weren't feeling well, and I wanted to stop by and check in."

The lie was so obvious, what with Ruby and Clifford standing just to his side, that it was laughable. But it did the trick and temporarily disarmed Cedric.

"Oh. Um, thanks for your concern."

"You don't look sick."

"It was just a stomach thing. I think I turned a corner for the better about an hour ago."

"So you're going back to work?"

"No... I think it's best if I stay home and rest and drink some water. I'll be good as new in time for work tomo—"

"Great. If you're not doing anything, then we'd love to have a chat with you. Would you invite us inside?"

Cedric planted his feet and cast a furtive glance over his shoulder. "Er... I don't know if it's a great time. The house is a mess—"

"Must be going around," Clifford said.

"—and I just ran out of tea to serve, so I would be a poor host."

Zax's grin stretched wider until he was practically

baring his teeth. "That's not a problem. We just had a hot drink before we came. And besides, we'd *really* like to talk to Opal."

At that, Cedric's eyes grew wide, and Ruby felt a strange pride for Zax's bold move to catch the other werebear by surprise. Maybe coffee made him bold and blunt too. Maybe they could spend more time in the near future drinking coffee together and causing trouble around town...

Sheesh, the coffee was even giving her bold *thoughts*. And completely useless ones, at that.

"Opal?" Cedric sputtered, trying to recover. "Why would she be here?"

Ruby decided to answer that. "Because the two of you are sleeping together. I thought that would be obvious."

Zax licked his lips, presumably in a desperate attempt to keep from laughing, and Cedric's next words caught in his throat, emerging finally as a garbled mess.

Finally, he managed, "How do you—I mean, where did you hear that?"

"Dear man," she said, "not only did I hear it through thick glass, but I saw it with my own eyes. Now I suggest you and Opal speak with us so things don't look even worse for you."

Cedric swallowed, his sand-colored face flushing red, and finally stepped to the side.

Zax nodded to him as he passed, and Ruby thanked him kindly. No one loved having a hellhound in their home, she was acutely aware of that, but they had Cedric by the snout now, and he didn't protest in the slightest as Clifford trotted past him.

Opal was wrapped in a silk dressing gown when she peeked her head out of the kitchen and saw who was waltzing into Cedric's living room. She appeared appropriately horrorstruck when Ruby said hello and asked her to join them.

"They know," Cedric groused right before he threw himself down onto a plaid wingback chair. Opal approached him cautiously and perched on the arm of his chair, taking in the newcomers with big doe eyes.

No one offered them anything as they sat, but Ruby didn't mind.

"We just visited your home," Ruby said, starting things off.

Opal's wide eyes narrowed. "You did?"

"Oh yes, and now we're very curious, as you might expect, what you were looking for in there."

Opal's attention jumped to Zax before landing on Ruby again. "What do you mean?"

"Someone was clearly searching for something in that home. Either that, or someone was in the mood to destroy all your possessions. Maybe you can enlighten us on what the case may be?"

Opal's mouth had fallen open, and she blinked, but said nothing.

"It wasn't you?" Ruby asked, feeling suddenly unsure.

"Someone was in my home?" Opal finally managed to force out.

"Oh yes," Ruby said. "And ransacked it. Did quite a number. My assumption was that you were looking for something."

Opal shook her head promptly. "No. I haven't been

back there since... Well, I suppose the secret's out. I haven't been back there in a couple of days."

"Ah, the sleepover was too fun, I suppose."

"No! It's not that. It's just that... We saw Taurus. Virgil was attacked. And Swamy... He went into the woods and never came out. I can only assume he's dead."

"I believe there are other assumptions still available to you if you so choose. But while we're on the topic of your boyfriend, I'd love to know when you last saw him."

Opal opened her mouth to respond, but Zax cut in. "When you *really* last saw him."

She exchanged a nervous glance with Cedric and paused before speaking. "I told you he didn't come home after work on Tuesday. But the truth is that I didn't see him before he went to work, either."

"The day before, then?" asked Zax.

"Yes. The morning before. Monday. I saw him then."

"And you stayed over here that night?"

"No!" she said, sounding scandalized.

Ruby only just managed not to groan. They were well past propriety at this point.

Opal continued, "I saw him before he left for work on Monday. Then I left for work. My shift ran long and then, yes, I did spend a little extra time with Cedric afterward. By the time I got home, it was late, and I thought it best to sleep on the couch rather than waking up Swamy."

"You mean," Ruby said politely, "you decided to sleep on the couch to avoid waking him and letting him know what time you really got home. If he slept through your arrival, you could fudge the time, say you made it home at a reasonable hour for someone working late at the lodge rather than tip him off to your nightly hobbies."

Opal looked suddenly murderous, and Ruby straightened up in her seat on the couch. Next to her, Clifford's hackles rose.

"Yes." Opal's tone was clipped. "I suppose that's what I mean."

"And you didn't see him Tuesday morning before he left for work?"

"No."

Ruby sighed. "Since I've just seen your home and am familiar with the layout, I find it hard to believe you slept right through his morning preparations while you were on the couch so close by. Did he not eat breakfast? Fix himself coffee?"

"I'm a sound sleeper," she said gruffly.

"And you'd had an exhausting night, I get that. But is it possible that Swamy didn't wake you up the next morning because he was never there? I assume you didn't check when you made it home to ensure he was safely asleep in his bed."

"I didn't. And I guess it's possible."

Ruby nodded. "And where exactly did your rendezvous take place on Monday night?"

Now both Cedric and Opal looked properly embarrassed. Well, that was a small consolation. "We met," Cedric said, chivalrously stepping in front of the bullet, "in one of the rooms of the lodge."

Zax growled. "Your boss will want to know about this."

Ruby placed a hand on his bulging bicep to calm him.

He could handle that sort of detail work later. There were more pressing matters on hand.

She addressed Cedric. "And where did you go afterward?"

"Straight home."

"And can anyone verify that?"

He sighed. "No. I live alone. And I don't think Virgil saw me."

"You're right. On Monday night, he was busy being attacked in the Silent Reach and then hiding in his bedroom with a battle hammer." She turned to Opal. "And you?"

"I went straight home, too."

"And I assume no one can verify that, either."

She shook her head, her arms crossed tightly like a petulant child. "Obviously not."

"That's unfortunate for you two, then." Ruby paused. "Were you aware that on the same night that you worked late and paid a visit to Cedric, Swamy had made plans with Virgil to track Taurus in the woods?"

Opal's gasp made it clear this was news to her. "I closed with Virgil that night. He never mentioned anything about *that*."

"Of course not. Why would anyone mention that they were dashing half-cocked into the woods after a legendary creature that is, at best, poorly defined?"

Cedric shook his head disappointedly. "That's just like Virgil. Talk about someone who could use a woman in his life."

Ruby couldn't stop herself. "If only we knew of a woman who had showed interest in him." She grinned pleasantly at Opal, whose murderous glare only intensified.

Cedric, though, didn't catch on, which was just fine.

Zax slapped his knees before standing. "We won't take up any more of your time." They made for the front door, Cedric close on their heels, herding them along.

Once on the doorstep, Zax turned around and called over Cedric's shoulder, "You should take care, Opal. There might be a murderer on the loose."

And Ruby didn't miss how Zax's eyes lingered on Cedric's for just a moment too long.

Chapter Seventeen

Bloom was exhausted as she climbed up Fluke Mountain. Not physically exhausted, thankfully, but mentally so. While she didn't need sleep, she regularly recharged with a recentering routine that involved deep breathing and a deep meditative state. But she hadn't had an opportunity to practice it in what seemed like days. No wait, maybe it *was* days.

She'd once heard Ruby sarcastically say, "I can sleep when I'm dead," and had always envied that claim. Sometimes, when the work got too tedious, Bloom envied the thought of not only sleeping, but being dead. A little finality sounded luxurious. As it was, neither sleep nor death made the cut on her long list of abilities, and she would just have to deal with it.

One thing she had no tolerance for, though, was hunger. Eating wasn't a requirement to her existence, but since leaving Heaven, she'd developed quite the addiction for food of all types, and when she went too long without it, she became cranky.

So when she entered Treetop Lodge and got her first divine whiff of a pan-seared steak, she hoped to goddess that she could find time during this meeting to order herself one.

She spotted Ruby and Zax across the restaurant. Both leaned forward with elbows on the table, and Ruby cradled a steaming teacup between her palms. Bloom paused, watching the two of them interact. She would definitely be the third wheel here. Ruby had had raw luck in love up to this point. Maybe Bloom ought to let things develop a little more between the flirtatious duo before she interrupted; when it came to eros, the presence of an angel could be tantamount to dousing someone in cold water.

There was really only one man in Eastwind who had found that particular quality of Gabby Bloom's attractive, and that relationship—if she would even call it that—had ended a century ago. That man was no good for her or anyone, but that was a whole different matter.

It was the lure of expertly cooked red meat that, in the end, drew her farther into the restaurant and over to Zax and Ruby's table.

"Oh, hello," Ruby said pleasantly, leaning back in her chair and taking a casual sip of her tea. "We were wondering if you'd be here at the time you set in your letter. We actually had a bet going. Zax thought you would be held up by police work, but I said you'd be right on the dot."

"I'm about thirty seconds late," Bloom said, not mentioning that it was a result of her hesitancy to interrupt the impromptu date.

"Still counts as on time," Ruby said. She turned to

Zax. "What'd I tell you? Never bet against Gabby Bloom."

Zax chuckled and nodded his concession. "You're right. I don't know what I was thinking." He turned to the sheriff. "Will you ever forgive me?"

"Only if you allow me to join you and order myself something bloody."

Ruby waved her off. "No need. I already ordered you a rare pan-seared steak with a side of scalloped potatoes and salted asparagus." She grinned. "Like I said, I knew you would be on time."

Bloom could have kissed her, but that would have fallen squarely under the list of bad third-wheel behaviors. "I guess it pays to be on time." She waved her wrist and a chair from the empty table next to theirs flew over to meet her. She took a seat and said, "I had an interesting interview with Arthur Flufferbum."

Ruby nodded politely. "And we had an interesting chat with Opal and Cedric. You go first."

Bloom filled them in on Arthur's refusal to give a hint as to his anonymous source, and Zax interjected, "I'm happy to go speak to him on behalf of the High Council."

"I'm sure you are. And I told him as much. It was only after I'd played that card that he gave me the scoop on this." She pulled out a copy of the article draft from Arthur's desk. "This will be running in the *Eastwind Watch* tomorrow morning, alongside a write-up about Swamy Stormstruck's disappearance."

She handed it first to Ruby, who read it over, nodding slowly, then handed it to Zax. As he read through it, she said, "Well, that makes sense of one thing."

"Does it?" said Bloom.

"Yes. If I'm not mistaken, and I don't believe I am, what I just read was a sampling of incriminating love letters between Opal Barker and Cedric Pine. Judging by the content, they seem to have been shared over a course of years. Years that Opal spent living with Swamy."

Zax folded up the sheet of paper, concern written in deep lines at the corners of his eyes. "There's going to be a lynch mob on Cedric's doorstep."

Bloom nodded.

But Ruby didn't seem to care so much about that. "There's something you don't know about yet, Sheriff."

"And that is?"

"Opal and Swamy's house was ransacked sometime in the last day or so."

Oh, that *was* interesting. She suspected she knew where Ruby was going. "The letters?"

"I believe so. Whoever sent the letters into the Watch was very likely the one who ransacked that house. But that means the person must have somehow known about the letters, but not known where they'd been moved. I guess whoever it was found them in the end."

"Or didn't find them," Bloom said. "Perhaps Opal went looking for them, knowing they were incriminating evidence against her lover. If they were already gone when she arrived, it would make sense for her to tear up the house looking for them."

"Except we already asked her about that. When we mentioned the state of the home, she looked genuinely confused."

"So you don't think it was her?"

"I do not."

"Then why don't you fill me in on the whole story?"

"Of course," Ruby said.

But before she could get another word out, Zax interrupted. "I'm sorry to dine and dash." He scooted his chair back from the table. "But I just noticed the time. I promised Count Malavic I would meet him to go over a budget proposal for tomorrow's High Council meeting, so I'd better take off."

"Right," Bloom said, derailed slightly by his sudden announcement. "Tell the Count I said hello, won't you?"

"Of course." He nodded at Ruby. "Ms. True, it's been a pleasure playing detective with you. Please keep me updated."

"Certainly. And tell the Count I also say hello." Ruby grinned. "He'll hate that."

Zax left, and Bloom returned her chair to its original table and took his seat; she hated having her back to the room.

"You know," Bloom mused, once Zax was out of earshot, "this investigation is messy, but at least we haven't once had to speak with Sebastian Malavic for it."

"True. It is rare that Eastwind's vampire-in-residence doesn't have his cold hands in the matter in some way, shape, or form."

Bloom grinned. "You would know all about those cold hands."

Ruby narrowed her eyes at the angel. "First off, that was years ago, and secondly, you're not without your own knowledge of them."

"But that was a hundred years ago, give or take a couple of decades. So much has happened since then."

Their waitress, Abigail Shoggins, approached, and Bloom ordered herself a glass of red wine.

"Drinking on duty?" said Ruby.

"Are you going to tell on me?"

"To whom?"

"Exactly. Besides, it would be a shame to eat the steak without the proper pairing."

"I won't fight with you on that." Ruby took a sip of her hot tea.

"Good. Now that you're done judging me, which we both know is my job anyway, how about you get on with your story?"

Ruby agreed and by the time she was finished relaying the conversation with the two prime suspects, Bloom's steak had arrived. "I have thoughts," she said, "but I also have steak, and this takes precedence."

The first cut sent a flood of delicious juices spilling onto her plate, mingling with the creamy potatoes and the butter from the asparagus. Her old comrades in Heaven really didn't know what they were missing. The meat practically melted in her mouth, and she moaned.

Ruby refilled her teacup from the small kettle in front of her. "Moaning at the taste of blood, huh? You know who you remind me of?"

Bloom, whose eyes had been closed, the better to savor the meal, opened them just enough to glare at her dinner companion. "You will not ruin this for me, no matter how hard you try."

"I wouldn't dream of it. Zax tells me they prepare this according to an old Wisconsin recipe. I already finished mine, so I can tell you that I firmly understand the emotion you're experiencing, and if you ever decide to take time off from work, I propose a ladies' trip to Wisconsin."

Once Bloom's food cravings had been adequately sated, she sat up straight, sighed, and said, "Okay, back to the case at hand. And yes, a trip to Wisconsin is happening at some point."

"It'd better be soon. I'm not getting any younger."

"True, but you're not exactly old, are you?"

"Of course not. But try telling that to my ankles first thing in the morning." Ruby paused. "Here's what I'm wondering." Bloom set down her utensils and paid Ruby her full attention. She could tell they were diving back in. "If Opal didn't tear up her home, who did?"

"That's really the question of the hour, isn't it?" replied Bloom. "Whoever tore up her home is likely the one who delivered the letters to Flufferbum. They must have known it would also put Cedric in a lot of danger."

"So do we have a case of vigilante justice? Maybe someone saw Cedric murder Swamy and is trying to make sure he doesn't get away with it."

"Or," Bloom said, "the real person behind Swamy's disappearance is trying to frame Cedric for it."

Ruby nodded. "It does seem like it's one or the other, doesn't it?"

"It does. Which we both know from hard-earned experience probably means there's a third possibility we're missing."

"And it's the correct one."

Bloom nodded. "What about Virgil? He's involved in this situation, even if it's not entirely clear why and how. And we can only take his word for the fact that his scratches were from Taurus or something like it and not from attacking and possibly killing Swamy in the woods that night. Perhaps Swamy *did* show up, after all. It's just a matter of taking Virgil's word."

"This is true," Ruby conceded. "His alibi is thin at best. Did you detect any guilt in him when we first spoke with him?"

Bloom nodded. "He was definitely withholding something, but now that I know more, it seems likely that it was the story of Opal kissing him and Swamy having possibly seen."

"Or maybe it was something more."

"Or maybe it was something more," Bloom echoed.

"The motive is something I don't understand, though. Why would he want to kill Swamy? There seems to be no reason."

It was something Bloom had considered in depth as well. "Perhaps Swamy's reason for getting Virgil out in the woods wasn't to hunt for Taurus but to hurt him for kissing Opal. And Virgil merely defended himself and in doing so killed Swamy."

"And hid the body?" Ruby asked.

Bloom frowned. "Right. I didn't detect that degree of guilt. Sure, it was clear he was hiding something relevant, but not something *that* relevant. And you know how everything anyone's ever done wrong tends to surface to the forefront of their mind when they speak with an angel."

"I don't, actually." Ruby sipped her tea.

"Not even a little?"

"Maybe years ago. But the more I learn about you, dear Gabby, the less I believe you actually have room to judge."

Bloom rolled her eyes and finished off the last of her wine.

From beside the table for two, Clifford's head shot up, and he looked toward the restaurant entrance a moment before a frantic figure sprinted in, her eyes wide as she scanned the restaurant. It was Opal Barker.

Her stare locked onto Bloom, then she rushed through the labyrinth of tables, shouting before she was even halfway there, "He's been attacked!"

"Who?" Bloom and Ruby asked at once.

"Cedric! He's been attacked!"

Gabby hurried to her feet. "When? By whom?"

"Just now," Opal said breathlessly as diners at the nearby tables gaped unabashedly at the scene. "It was Taurus. Taurus attacked him."

Ruby said, "Lead the way."

"Yes," said Bloom, wondering how a being that didn't exist managed to wreak so much havoc. "Lead the way."

Chapter Eighteen

A million possible scenarios raced through Ruby's mind as she and Clifford hurried after Bloom and Opal. But none of them, at least by her accounting of the facts, actually included Taurus, the legendary werebear bane himself, attacking Cedric in broad daylight. It just didn't make any sense.

And yet, Opal blathered on about it in a nonsensical and panicked flow, and Sheriff Bloom placated her with plenty of nods and halfhearted sounds of understanding.

Finally, they reached the spot. It was one Ruby had already walked today, as it wasn't far from Opal's home.

They found Cedric sitting on the ground, leaning against a boulder just off the footpath. He clutched as many of his wounds as he could.

"Siren's song," cursed Ruby under her breath as she took in the severity of his gashes.

Blood dripped down his forehead from a single cut just below his hairline, and his forearms both held defensive wounds similar to the ones on Virgil. On top of all that, there seemed to be a great amount of blood flowing down Cedric's right side. He moaned and tried to call out to Bloom, but his speech was slurred.

"He saved me," Opal said. "He saved me from Taurus."

Bloom knelt in front of him and grimaced slightly. It was fortunate that the angel had enjoyed her bloody steak *before* this incident. Was she imagining it now?

"Zax," Ruby said. "I'll send an owl. Maybe he hasn't made it to his meeting with Malavic yet, and he can hurry back with some of the ointment he used on Virgil."

Bloom nodded her approval decisively and then returned to her scan of Cedric's wounds. Ruby knew he wouldn't die, so long as Bloom was with him—she had tricks up her sleeve to keep people alive—but she was no healer.

Clifford trotted beside Ruby as she ran to the nearest home to borrow (without asking) their owl. A brown spotted owl napped on the perch above its bell, just to the side of the front door, and Ruby searched deep into her pockets for what she needed. Her fingertips found a bit of charcoal and a scrap of parchment from an old grocery list. That would do.

She scribbled, *Attack on Cedric. Head toward Opal's home. Bring ointment.* Then she told the owl who to locate and watched it fly away. How long would it take for Zax to arrive?

Bloom would need her. Not to help Cedric, but to manage Opal, who had been on the verge of hysterics.

And nothing had changed by the time Ruby returned. "Come with me over here, dear," Ruby said in her calmest most matronly tone. She put an arm around

Opal's waist because the woman's shoulders were a foot too tall for her and led her away from the messy scene.

Once they were far enough away that Cedric's moans were mostly inaudible, Ruby said, "Tell me what happened."

Opal's voice shook, and her eyes were still wide, her pupils so dilated none of her green irises could be seen. But she managed to answer, and Ruby was grateful for that. "After you left, I told Cedric I wanted to go see my home, to see how big the mess was and try to put it back together. He fought me on it. He said what had happened there was a crime, someone was desperate. And it would be stupid to return to the scene of the crime." Her taut expression drooped into misery. "And he was right."

Ruby's Insight was gently nudging her in the sternum, and she told it, *Yes, I know. The letters.* But now didn't seem like the right time to interrogate Opal about that. "I assume you convinced him to change his mind?"

"Yes. Only after an argument, though. He needed a little time to cool down, but finally he said it must mean a lot to me, and if I had to go, he would come with me." She put her head in her hands, making the last of her words difficult to hear. "I should have listened to him. None of this would have happened."

Ruby leaned forward and patted the hunched-over Opal on the shoulder. "Now, now. He's going to be just fine. It looks bad now, yes, but Zax Banderfield is on the way, and we'll get him all fixed up."

Opal hiccupped and raised her head. "He saved me. If he hadn't come with me, I don't know what would have happened. Taurus might have killed me!"

Ruby had her doubts about that but spoke nothing of them. "He's a very brave man, that's for sure. But he's also tough. I'm sure he'll be back on his feet in no time."

Just then, Zax appeared around the bend, hustling over at a solid jog. "Oh, thank goddess," Ruby moaned, and went to meet him by Cedric and Bloom.

Along with the ointment from the Pixie Mixie, Zax had smartly brought with him a roll of bandages and a small flagon of water.

Well, wasn't he just the prepared one? Ruby appreciated people who were quick on their feet when the swirls hit the fan.

There was no more discussion of what had happened for the ten minutes that followed. Once the blood was washed away, the wounds didn't look nearly as intimidating. The damage was likely not even life threatening. While Ruby guessed he would have a scar on his forehead and a few on his forearms, the scratches on his side were hardly more than superficial, despite having produced so much blood.

Before he declared his patient fixed, Zax reached in his back pocket and pulled out a small flask, handing it off to Cedric. "Whiskey," he said.

Cedric took it gladly and knocked back two swigs before he returned it to his sleuth leader. "Thanks."

"Can you tell us what happened now?" Ruby asked.

But Bloom interrupted. "Hold on." She looked over her shoulder to where Opal was standing, clutching herself. "Would you mind having a seat on that bench over there while we talk to him?"

Opal narrowed her eyes at the sheriff. "Why?"

"I don't want you to have to relive it."

The lie was more transparent than any ghost Ruby had ever seen, but Opal apparently had bigger concerns preoccupying her. "But what if he's still out there?"

"Clifford will go with you," Bloom said. "That okay, Cliff?"

"On it, Sheriff," he said dutifully, and went to stand by Opal.

While Bloom couldn't hear his reply, he'd made himself clear, and she turned back to Cedric once Opal was out of the way. "Okay, now you can tell us what happened."

The fact that Bloom was intent on splitting the couple up meant that both Opal and Cedric were still firmly on her suspect list. And they couldn't have two suspects overhearing each other's account of the attack. It would have tainted the evidence.

And that also indicated that Bloom still wasn't buying the Taurus nonsense either.

Cedric's breathing was labored, but he pushed through the pain to respond. "Opal insisted on going back to her house to check on it after she heard it'd been torn apart. I didn't want her to go for obvious reasons of her safety, but she insisted, so I went with her. Then, I heard a rustle in the woods just back there"—he pointed—"but I figured it was just a deer or something. Maybe even a few birds flapping around in the bushes. That was until the cursed thing stepped out." He shuddered. "It was huge. It looked right at me and then charged."

"Right at you, or right at the both of you?" Bloom asked.

"Just me."

"Do you think it had you singled out, then?"

He held up his bandaged arm where the blood was already soaking through. "Yeah, I'd say so."

"Did you get the sense," Ruby asked, "that Opal was in any danger at all?"

Cedric considered it and then said, "Only if she'd tried to step between Taurus and me."

"How big would you say it was?" Bloom asked.

Cedric shrugged and looked around vaguely.

"Zax," Bloom said, turning to the sleuth leader. "Would you stand to give us some sort of reference point?"

The werebear looked at her askance but did as she requested.

"Taller or shorter than Zax?" Bloom prompted.

"Um, well... probably about the same height."

"So it *was* tall then," said Bloom. "Zax is no dwarf."

Zax nodded. "I come from big stock," he said proudly, taking a knee in front of Cedric again.

"What happened then?" Bloom asked. "What made him leave rather than finishing the job, you think?"

Cedric cringed. "I think he assumed he *did* finish the job. After he got me in the side and across the head, I'm a little embarrassed to say I went down. I would've gotten back up to protect Opal, but it didn't seem necessary. He turned and ran down the path."

Bloom's eyebrows shot up. "He ran down the path? Not straight back into the woods?"

"No. Down the path. That way." He pointed.

"Perhaps," said Ruby, "he wanted to be seen." She exchanged a look with Bloom before the angel cast a glance over her shoulder at Clifford. The hellhound was on his feet, prowling a tight protective circle around Opal.

Ruby knew then what they were about to do, and while her survival instincts weren't all too thrilled with it, she did love a bit of danger.

Nothing like risking death to make one appreciate being alive.

Bloom turned to Zax. "I don't want to keep you from your meeting with Malavic. You know how broody he gets when he's bored. We'll take it from here."

Zax got to his feet slowly. "You sure?"

"Yes," replied the sheriff. "With my powers, Ruby's Insight, and Clifford's teeth, I think we can manage ourselves fine." Her smile was polite, but clearly a dismissal.

"All right then," he said, casting Ruby a concerned glance. She nodded at him, hoping to convey that she appreciated his chivalrous consideration but agreed with Bloom's directive.

Once Zax was out of sight, Ruby and Bloom each grabbed Cedric under an armpit and helped raise him slowly to his feet. "Let's get you two somewhere safe," Bloom said. "We'll be back to check on you later. But first, Ms. True and I have something that demands our urgent attention."

Chapter Nineteen

Clifford's nose bounced so rapidly just a half-inch above the dirt foot path that it almost looked like he was having a seizure. But experience informed Sheriff Bloom that this was quite usual for the hellhound. Not only that, but this was him in his element, getting to sniff out a trail that undoubtedly led straight to danger.

They'd dropped Opal and Cedric off at Opal's home where she could begin to straighten the mess and Cedric could rest.

Only an hour before, she would have thought leaving the two of them together could be putting Opal's life in danger, but now she wasn't so sure. If Cedric *was* responsible for the attack on his brother and Swamy's disappearance and possibly, perhaps even likely, murder, he was likely too injured to do any real damage to Opal, who was by no means a tiny woman herself.

But now that he'd been attacked, Bloom's firm suspicion had become unstuck. Unless he somehow staged them, he was probably not the one behind his and

Virgil's attacks. There was someone involved in all this whom they hadn't properly investigated, and he was slowly crawling to the top of her list.

But her new theory was still too fresh to get attached to.

And besides, they would likely learn much more once they found where this trail was leading.

"Any indication of species?" Bloom asked.

"Cliff says it smells like a werebear. But he adds the caveat that everything in this area of Eastwind smells like werebear."

"Any particular werebear?"

"He can't say yet. There are a few familiar scents running this way."

The path split, with the branch on the right running parallel along the lane of homes that continued up the mountain. The other branch twisted off deeper into the woods.

Without missing a beat, Clifford went into the woods.

"Huh," said Ruby.

"What?"

"He says there are three distinct scents that he recognizes going this way. But he can't tell which one is fresher than the others."

Bloom was getting impatient. The sun was beginning to set, and the dark canopy of the woods swallowed them up. "And to whom do these familiar scents belong?"

Ruby was silent for a moment, no doubt carrying on with her familiar. Finally, once they were fifty yards farther down the path, she said, "Keep in mind there are others in here, but only three are familiar to him. Virgil, Zax, and Swamy."

"Swamy?" Bloom said. "How does he know Swamy's scent?"

"When we stopped by his home. Clifford stayed outside, but he says there was a scent all around that he took to be Swamy's because it wasn't Opal's. He smells the same one now mixed in with the rest."

"I think we ought to follow that one, if it comes to choosing," Bloom said.

"And if it doesn't come to choosing, we've found ourselves in quite a messy situation."

Bloom couldn't agree more.

She should have requested that Clifford go along with Deputy Titterfield on his original search. They'd wrangled in a good number of werebears for it, and even a few werewolves, and while their sense of smell was far better than, say, hers, it didn't hold a candle to the scenting abilities of a hellhound. Maybe if Clifford had come earlier, they could have discovered Swamy's body sooner and put this case to rest.

But it had all seemed so small at first. The search was more of a formality to allay Opal's fear than because Bloom thought Swamy was in any grave danger. He'd hardly been missing twenty-four hours (or so they thought at the time) when the search had gone out. Bloom had seen a lot of similar situations over the years, and almost all of them resolved themselves in an anticlimactic way—the missing person simply returned after a little time away with a very sound and often obvious reason why they had left in the first place.

Nothing about this, initially at least, indicated it wouldn't be filed away with all of those cases.

And yet, she was wrong. It was a strange part of being law enforcement for centuries; her rational mind, using the data of her many encounters, almost always told her that the odds of something being terribly remiss were low, while her gut, or perhaps her elevated nervous system, always thought the worst-case scenario was just around the corner. Balancing the paradox was the trick. Knowing when to lean one way or another was a skill she hadn't yet mastered and probably never would.

But pretending she had it all under control, that was something she was great at. It helped that people naturally assumed an angel would be in control of the situation, let alone one who was also the sheriff. All she had to do was keep from convincing anyone otherwise.

Clifford stopped in his tracks, letting out a low and muffled growl.

Not even Gabby Bloom was immune to the foreboding sensation of watching a hellhound go on high alert. "What is it?" she whispered to Ruby.

"He smells blood."

"Fresh?"

There was a pause, then Ruby said, "Either a small amount of fresh blood or a large amount of dried blood."

"Does he know who it belongs to?"

"No. He doesn't know their blood scent. All three scents are still present on this trail."

Bloom nodded. "Let's keep going."

They did, but there were no more new developments, and ten minutes later they turned a sharp corner, and then another and ended at the edge of a creek.

"We must have found our way to the Silent Reach," Bloom said.

"And this is the creek Virgil mentioned, I'd bet," Ruby added.

The sheriff sighed. "Then we've hit a dead end."

"I hope you only mean that figuratively."

Before Bloom could respond, something large moved on the other side of the creek. The sheriff only spotted it in her peripheral vision, and by the time she looked directly at it, it had stopped moving. She couldn't make it out as well through the twilit gloom of the woods. Maybe she had just imagined it.

Except, no, because Ruby and Clifford were looking in the exact same direction. The hellhound snorted before his nose began twitching manically again.

And then the thing moved, and Bloom only just managed to keep from gasping.

Because it *was* large, even at this distance she could tell that. From paw to the top of its horns, it easily had a foot on her.

It was one thing to hear the descriptions of Taurus from unreliable witnesses, but it was a completely different thing to see the beast, or at least its massive silhouette, with her own eyes. The descriptions she'd heard before made much more sense—not just the words, but the emotions behind them.

If she didn't know better, she might have believed them all now.

But the goddess didn't give her a brain just so she could disregard it.

With the legs of the werebear, the body of a man, and the head of a bull, Bloom knew this particular creature didn't exist. That didn't stop the goosebumps from overtaking her arms at the sight of it, but it did stop her from falling into the same narrative trap that had ensnared its previous victims.

"Eastwind Sheriff," she called out to it. "I just want to speak with you."

As she'd expected, the figure took off deeper into the woods.

Clifford relaxed once it was gone and even walked closer to the stream to take a sip.

"Well, isn't that something?" Ruby said.

"It sure is. Seems a little strange that a resurrected legendary were-killer would flee at the first sign of law enforcement."

Ruby chuckled. "It does indeed. So what do we do now?"

Bloom considered it. "The only way we can catch whoever that is, is to sit on the next intended target. and wait."

"And who do you propose?"

"Opal Barker."

Ruby raised an eyebrow. "But she could easily have been attacked earlier, and Cedric said the attacker didn't even look at her."

"I know. But I'm not sure whoever this is wants to see her injured, although I can almost guarantee you there will be a confrontation as soon as he or she can get Opal alone. And when that happens, one of us ought to be there."

Chapter Twenty

Opal had done an admirable job of cleaning her home, and it freed up Ruby to relax once she got there. In fact, this stakeout might prove nothing more than a great opportunity for the Fifth Wind to have a little peace and quiet and get some reading done.

Ruby sat in a wooden rocking chair, a candle on a small table next to her providing just enough light in the dark bedroom for her to make out the words of *Romantically A Were.* Clifford snoozed at her feet, close enough that she could stick her toes underneath him to keep them nice and toasty while she read.

Her familiar had remained awake and alert for the first two hours of their watch, but it was well past his bedtime now, and he'd succumbed to the allure of sleep. She couldn't blame him. For one, he couldn't have a cup of tea to keep him awake like she could. But for another, he was already well past the usual life expectancy for a hellhound. That was part of the gig with familiars, though. When she'd met him upon arriving in Eastwind, he suspected, though he couldn't be sure, that he was a couple of years old. Twenty years later, and he had aged much more slowly, adapting to her lifespan rather than his own. If what she'd read and been told by others was true, he could live for another sixty years if she made it that long, though by that point he might have a body more like a what one would expect from a senior dog. But she would have a body like what one would expect from a senior Fifth Wind, so, fair enough.

Long before then, however, she would be too old to do this sort of thing, this stakeout. That is, if she wasn't already. That part was up in the air, considering she vacillated so furiously between being ready for bed at 9 p.m. and staying up half the night with a complete inability to catch a wink. The latter was a new part of her life, and she suspected it might stick around for the next few years.

But the sleeplessness came in handy tonight. Even as she read a book in the dimness, she felt as alert as could be. Perhaps that was adrenaline, but perhaps it was the other thing, the one she didn't want to name because not only did no one talk about it, but she thought naming it might jinx it. And jinxes were a genuine concern in Eastwind.

She looked over at the peaceful figure in the bed, her chest rising and falling slowly beneath the light quilt. Must be nice to rest so soundly at the drop of a hat.

They'd carted Cedric off to his own house for the night and told him not to leave under any circumstances. She wondered if he was sleeping soundly or if his wounds were keeping him awake.

Ruby felt a sweat coming on, and pulled her toes out from under Clifford, hoping that was all it was.

Nope. As soon as she did so, her feet were cold again, and the rest of her was still a little toasty.

It was just as she tried to shimmy her toes back underneath her familiar that she heard heavy footsteps.

Clifford's ears were up in a millisecond.

She held her breath.

"Where are they coming from?" she asked.

"Front porch."

This was it. The moment to test her's and Bloom's theory. Was someone hoping to sneak up on Opal? She'd been sure to leave the front door unlocked to allow easier entry so she could unmask whoever it was without him or her getting deterred.

Who's there? she called out, but only in her mind.

She had a few ideas who it might be. The day's events had certainly helped narrow her focus.

She nodded for Clifford to follow her out into the hallway.

For a beast so large, he was deadly silent on his feet. Not for the first time, she was glad the only hellhound she encountered in her day-to-day was one she was forever bonded to and therefore one who wouldn't try to eat her. And she was also grateful that the rest of Clifford's kind stayed put in the Deadwoods.

But whoever was on the front porch wasn't so light on his feet.

There was the softest tap on the door, and Ruby paused at the edge of the hallway, taking a quick step back to shield herself behind the corner of the wall where she couldn't be seen from the front door.

Another soft tap.

Huh. That was strange. Was the intruder testing to see if he could get Opal to answer the door? Perhaps he had plans to pull her out into the night. Maybe he thought knocking could have alerted the neighbors.

It was late, but not quite the dead of night. Those who didn't have to be up at dawn for work might still be lounging around, enjoying a good book or the company of each other.

"Should I answer it?" Ruby asked.

"I don't suspect you'll have to."

And sure enough, Clifford was right, because a moment after the knock, the doorknob began to turn.

Ruby held her breath, wondering where the best place to hide would be if it came to it. She doubted it would come to that, though—Clifford was a force to be reckoned with, even for someone as large as the figure she'd seen in the woods.

Still, she hated the thought of Clifford going into combat. There was always the chance of injury or worse. What would she do without him?

"Take a step back," she instructed just as the hellhound was creeping closer to the front door.

"I'm not exactly compact. Whoever it is will see me no matter where I try to hide."

"Yet again, you blur the lines between bravery and recklessness."

The front door opened like a whisper.

She felt the cool night air on her face before she could make out the figure in the doorway.

He looked even larger now than he had in the woods.

Except one thing was different.

He didn't have a bull's head.

He stepped forward, and Ruby pressed herself to the wall on the other side of the corner. Her heart raced. Was this a half-baked plan? It had seemed so good when they'd concocted it earlier.

The intruder spoke in a low whisper. "Ruby? You here?"

Ruby's breath caught in her chest. She recognized that voice. But it couldn't be. And *he* couldn't be.

Clifford's low growl gave away their poor hiding place, and Ruby steadied herself before stepping out behind her familiar.

Zax Banderfield stood just inside the threshold, glaring down at her through the gloom.

Chapter Twenty-One

"I can't believe it," Ruby said. "You. This whole time."

Zax stepped closer, and she took a quick step back as Clifford bared his teeth. The werebear stopped in his tracks and looked down at the hellhound with alarm.

And, unless the shadows from the moon streaming through the window were misleading her, there was confusion in his expression as well.

"What do you mean?" Zax said. Then he groaned and held up his hands, the gesture of an innocent man on the defensive. "No, you got it all wrong."

"Oh, do I? I'm not so sure. You're sneaking into the house of the missing person, the house of a woman who was in close contact with an attack just today."

"I know it looks bad—"

"Then you're not an idiot, at least." That shut him up, and she was able to continue. "Clifford smelled your scent heading to the Silent Reach. I totally dismissed it, but... Why did you do it?"

"I didn't!"

The loudness of his voice felt crass in the quiet home, and she flinched.

"I didn't," he repeated, this time a whisper. "If you'd just let me explain."

Clifford growled again.

"And call off the dog, please."

Ruby said, "He's not a dog."

"You bet your hide, I'm not!"

A pleading in Zax's eyes reached out and touched the part of her heart that would do anything to keep this betrayal from being a reality.

"For fang's sake," she muttered, disappointed with herself. Then, *"Okay, Cliff. Give him some space."*

Clifford tucked his teeth away beneath his heavy jowls and backed a step closer to his witch.

"Tell me why you're here and make it quick."

Zax didn't hesitate. "I thought you'd be here."

"And? What were you intending?"

There was one thing she would have liked for him to say, and another (murder) that she was dreading.

"I was intending—I *am* intending to help keep you safe. This is a dangerous idea. Whoever attacked Virgil and Cedric and Swamy could be coming here next."

"Yes," she said, losing patience, "that's the idea."

"And all you have to keep you safe is Clifford?"

"He made you back off, didn't he?"

Zax grunted. "Yes, but—"

"You don't know me that well," she said, a sneaking suspicion forming. "What made you think I would do this?" Before he could answer, she took a stab at it. "It was Malavic, wasn't it? You filled him in on news from the mountain, mentioned I was involved, and he guessed

I would be doing something like this." Only the vampire, in his perpetually bored and therefore calculating state of mind would have stumbled upon this scenario. And been completely correct.

"Yes, okay," Zax admitted begrudgingly. "He mentioned that this would be something you and Bloom would think up."

"How do I know you're telling the truth? You were unaccounted for when Cedric was attacked this afternoon."

Now Zax seemed to be losing patience. "Why would I attack someone and then immediately bandage him up? It makes no sense!"

"Maybe you didn't have a choice."

"I had a choice with Virgil, and I dragged my hide into town to get him supplies at the Pixie Mixie. I'm the sleuth leader. They're all under my care. Why would I have done any of this?" He risked a step closer, and this time Clifford didn't growl.

"It all revolves around Opal, doesn't it? Perhaps her secret relationships extend beyond Cedric."

He caught her insinuation immediately. "No way. She's not even a little bit my type."

"No?"

"No." He inched closer. He was only a few feet from the corner of the hallway. "She's still in her twenties. I like women more my age. And I like them smarter. And smaller."

Ruby cleared her throat. "Maybe we ought to take this discussion into the bedroom." When he arched an eyebrow at her, she hastened to add, "To keep an eye on my ward. If you're not the one I'm waiting for, then he or she could show up at any minute."

"Right. Of course."

"*Smooth,*" Clifford said.

"*Oh, please.*"

Ruby entered the room first and peeked at the woman beneath the heavy blankets. The conversation in the living room hadn't roused her, so the plan was technically still a go.

To say that things turning out this way with Zax was a relief was a gross understatement. In fact, it was actually better this way. Now she had even more protection against whoever might show up to get a final word in with Opal.

Ruby took a seat in the chair again and watched as Zax looked around only to discover that there was nowhere left for him to sit. "Settle in," she whispered, nodding toward the spot on the woven rug next to her.

His eyes flicked down to Clifford, who had already settled in at Ruby's feet. "I'm fine standing." He crossed his arms and leaned against the wall. "So, do we just wait until someone comes creeping—"

The quiet but unmistakable click of the front door shutting cut him off. Ruby's eyes went wide, and she pointed frantically at the closet just to the left of where Zax leaned against the wall.

There was no way the three of them would all fit, so as Clifford slinked back into the shadows in the corner of the room, Ruby and Zax squeezed into the closet, trying desperately to keep the hangers from clattering against each other as they did.

She closed the closet door, peering through the wooden slats, waiting to see who entered.

Ruby was keenly aware of Zax's warm arm pressed against hers. And though the proximity was making her a little lightheaded, and she had a strong impulse to grab his hand for security, she refrained.

The soft and slow footfalls coming down the hallway were those of someone determined not to be heard.

Only a moment later, and the bedroom door slid open with the faintest squeak of rusty hinges. The sound sent shivers down Ruby's spine.

And then, finally, the figure stepped forward, and she was able to see who it was. Zax must have gotten his first look, too, because she felt him stiffen beside her. She looked up at him, the moonlight from the window at the head of the bed slipping between the slats and casting stripes of pale blue across his face. She held a finger to her lips, and he nodded.

Taurus paused just feet from the foot of the bed, his stature even more imposing now than it had been in the woods.

"Hold your position," she called to Clifford, sensing his anticipation mingling with her own.

She needed the newcomer to be so locked in that he would be caught off guard when she put the next part of the plan into action, but she dared not wait too long and risk him attacking his final target. Not that his final target was at all defenseless herself...

Before he moved closer, though, his hands raised toward his head, and he grabbed both sides, just under the horns.

The bull's head slipped right off, and he cradled it under one armpit as he stared down at the bed.

And the last piece of her theory clicked into place.

Swamy Stormstruck wasn't dead. He wasn't even missing.

He was Taurus.

And when the realization struck Zax, who gasped, things had to happen very quickly after that.

Chapter Twenty-Two

Ruby cursed just as Swamy's head whirled around to face the closet where Zax had just given away their position.

She shut her eyes tightly and psychically inhaled. Though her eyes remained shut, she knew from experience that the room would be pitch black. It had taken years of practice, but now she could Quench even moonlight in a small enough space.

This blackness wasn't darkness. It was heavy like a lead blanket. No light could penetrate it, and only two types of beings could see through it: the Fifth Wind who created it and the familiar who belonged to her.

And that was all that she needed.

Clifford sprang, tackling Swamy to the floor with a heavy thud.

Ruby let go of her breath and the moonlight returned just long enough for her ward to jolt up in bed.

Sheriff Gabby Bloom, no doubt refreshed from her long meditation, shot glowing golden ties from her hands.

Her aim was true, but Ruby had never seen her miss her target.

The golden restraints hobbled Swamy and pulled his hands together behind his back. One more flick of the angel's wrist, and he was properly hogtied.

Clifford stepped off cautiously, just enough to allow Bloom to get out of bed and grab his bindings. She slid the werebear belly-down across the wood floor and then heaved him up and onto the bed.

Goddess, the woman's strength was terrifying. Sure, she was fit and toned, but she was slim. Nothing about the circumference of her biceps spoke to that degree of strength.

"Thanks for joining us, Mr. Stormstruck," she said, grinning down at him where he lay on his side, struggling against his restraints. "Your appearance has made my day. I just solved a bunch of cases all at once."

Ruby cleared her throat from where she now stood just outside the confines of the closet.

"Oh, right," Bloom said. "*We* just solved a bunch of cases."

"Where's Opal?" Swamy demanded.

"Nowhere you can find her," Bloom said. "We made sure of that."

"I just wanted to talk to her!"

Clifford scented the air. *"Does anyone else smell unicorn swirls? Just me?"*

Ruby chuckled then addressed Swamy. "If you just wanted to talk to her, you could have done that a long time ago. You know, when you two lived together. Before you decided to start going after every man she ever laid hands on."

"If I'd done that," he said, his tone souring, "there'd hardly be a werebear on this mountain who wasn't worse for the wear."

"That seems like an exaggeration," Zax muttered.

"Defensive, huh? What, you get with her, too?"

Zax rolled his eyes. "If I had, there wouldn't be a thing you could do about it. It's my right as sleuth leader. But also, no thanks. She's all yours. Well, yours and Cedric's."

Swamy spat at him, and Zax stepped back just in time to avoid the splatter on his boot.

"Virgil," Ruby said, stepping forward. "You saw her and Virgil in the restaurant that night, didn't you?"

"You bet your hide, I did! She'd been working late so much, well past when anyone else worked. She'd come home after midnight, sneak in, clean up, and sleep on the couch. She thought I didn't hear her come in, but I did. And I saw what time it was. I knew something was up."

"So you finally decided to drop into her work to check it out?"

He scowled. "And I'm glad I did. I saw her with that Pine jerk and knew immediately what I had to do. I couldn't keep her from running around on me, that much was clear, but I could make her and every man who laid his filthy paws on her sorry for what he'd done."

"Why Taurus?" Ruby asked. She was already formulating a theory, but she wanted to hear it from his own lips.

"It was too easy, wasn't it? Everyone's already heard the story, everyone has that deeply ingrained fear. And nothing is easier to feed than that. All I had to do was drop a few mentions here and there throughout the sleuth, and the story took on a life of its own. Sure, I took liberty with some of the descriptions, but I never pushed it too far. That idiot Virgil really believed it." Swamy chuckled. "He agreed to help me search for Taurus in the woods. It was almost too easy."

Zax whistled low, looking at Ruby and Bloom. "Still waters run deep."

"Turns out there's a whole whirlpool of crazy beneath the still surface," Clifford added.

"You can say that again."

Bloom took up the thread. "But Virgil got away. You didn't kill him."

"Kill him? I didn't want to kill him. I wanted him to live. To live in fear."

He'd really drunk his own potion, hadn't he? Ruby couldn't believe the mind on some people. "While I appreciate that you didn't add any spirits to my workload," she said, "I hardly think your lack of intention to kill your victims will lead to any sort of leniency when you face trial. After all, any of your inflicted injuries could have festered and took the victim's life. You're lucky that wasn't the case. Especially with Virgil."

"I don't regret it. Sure, it didn't turn out that he was the one spending all that alone time with Opal, but he did kiss her. He's guilty of that."

"When did you find out that it wasn't him?" Bloom asked.

"When I saw her and Cedric in the kitchen together. They were doing a lot more than kissing."

For a moment, Ruby did feel sorry for him. She, too, had been unfortunate enough to witness such a thing, and it was awful enough without either of the participants being someone she loved and thought she could trust.

"All food safety violations aside," Bloom said, "I think it's about time you come with me." She undid the tie securing his bound hands and hobbled ankles so he was able to straighten out.

And then there was that terrifying show of strength again as she pulled him to sitting on the bed. "You try to hop off, and you won't get far, understood?"

He muttered a response Ruby couldn't make out.

They followed the sheriff to the door where she paused and addressed them. "As always, Ruby, thanks for your help. And you, too, Mr. Banderfield. I'll touch base with you once I book this creep. In the meantime, be sure to give Clifford an extra sausage with his dinner."

Then a sly grin tugged at the corners of her lips as she looked from Ruby to Zax and back again. "And you two enjoy the rest of your night."

Chapter Twenty-Three

Clifford maintained a courteous distance behind Ruby and Zax on their walk back to Ruby's home. Despite her insistence that she would be safe traveling with her familiar at night, Zax wouldn't take no for an answer. At least not when it came to that. He had yet to test her *other* boundaries.

And she wasn't sure if no was even in her vocabulary for such things. Not when it came to him. Not after so long without. And not when her heart was still racing from the confrontation.

They reached the first step of her porch, and she half expected this to be where Zax stopped and said goodnight.

But it wasn't. The werebear followed her up the stairs of her attached cottage to her doorstep.

Was he expecting her to invite him in?

Was she planning on inviting him in?

If he asked, would she refuse?

She straightened up as much as she could to lessen

the height difference between them. "Thank you for chaperoning me."

"Thank you for tolerating it. I know it wasn't your first choice, but I wouldn't have been able to sleep if I wasn't sure you'd made it home safely."

"I'm not sure I'm going to be able to sleep tonight regardless," she replied.

He took a step closer, leaving almost no room between them. "Want company?"

Her stomach fluttered in a way she thought she'd long outgrown. "Yes, actually." She paused, already lamenting this decision. "But I think it's best if I have a little time to myself."

He nodded, a half-smile resting on his lips. "I had to try."

"I'm glad you did."

They stood silent for a moment, gazes locked on to one another's.

"Well, good night, Ruby. It's been a pleasure doing business with you."

Pleasure and business, the two things she knew not to mix. The thought sobered her a split second before he inched closer.

Oh goddess, was he going in for the kiss?

Please, please, please...

No! There are too many unknowns! Don't be a fool!

But while her head and heart were still locked in a heated debate, he wrapped his large arms around her and pulled her into his body.

Siren's song, did his warm and firm body feel pleasant! She didn't want the hug to stop, but it did a moment after he planted a soft kiss on the top of her head. "You take care of yourself." He made for the steps.

"Zax!"

He paused and cast her a look over his bulky shoulder.

Now what? His name had been out of her mouth before she'd known why. "If you ever find yourself in the presence of an unwanted spirit, you let me know."

"I don't know if I could afford you."

"I bet we could come to a mutually beneficial agreement."

He chuckled lightly as he disappeared down the dark street.

Ruby unlocked her front door and called for Clifford, who had been waiting patiently at the edge of the porch, to come inside.

The spirit of Mirna floated in the middle of her parlor, bobbing slowly, her arms folded across her chest. She was in just the spot Ruby'd left her that morning with the promise of being home soon.

As Mirna launched into it, Ruby sighed, "Not right now."

"You keep saying that! When will you actually follow through?" Mirna snapped.

"The morning."

"But you said—"

"And now I'm saying that if you even so much as *think about* haunting me in my dreams, I'll banish you straight to misery."

The ghost grumbled and muttered under her breath before slipping out of visibility. It was only temporary, though. Manifesting required energy, and some spirits had more of it to spare. When they were out, they simply disappeared into a nebulous dimension until they could rally again.

Yes, Ruby would definitely have to handle Mirna in the morning. She'd put it off long enough, running around with Bloom, and pretending things could be different for her...

The stark contrast between the warmth of Zax's embrace and the chill of the ghostly presence left Ruby unbelievably cranky and extremely exhausted. Maybe she *would* be able to sleep through the night. And maybe some sweet dreams would tide her over for another few years of solitude.

As her head hit the pillow only minutes later, Clifford settled himself down onto his soft dog bed by the window.

She closed her eyes and knew sleep was imminent. But before it could overtake her...

"I think he might be one of the good ones."

Ruby sighed. *"I guess we'll never know."*

"You confronted a maniac tonight without blinking an eye, and you're scared to get close to a werebear who insists on walking you to your doorstep and doesn't get mad when you send him on his way?"

"I'm not scared of it."

"Then what were you thinking?"

"You're suddenly very interested in my love life, aren't you?"

"Not suddenly. I've been here for all of it, and as your best friend, I'm telling you that if you don't go for it, you'll just be miserable and make my life miserable."

"So this is about you, in the end."

"I guess so, and why shouldn't it be? Someone's gotta look out for my happiness."

Ruby grunted and flopped over to her other side, suddenly uncomfortable in her current position. *"No one knows better than we do that romance only causes trouble. Nothing lasts. There are a limited number of ways it can play out, and none have happy endings. Either the romance ends, which is never easy, or it only ends for one person, who then seeks out greener pastures, like with Opal and Swamy. Or you die. Everything goes south in the end. I don't see the point of getting involved in it."*

"I think everything going south in the end is the best *reason to get involved. Nothing lasts. Take advantage of it while you can."*

Ruby didn't have a response to that, so she remained silent, considering it. But Clifford's soft snores interrupted her swirling thoughts before long, and, finally, she drifted off to sleep.

Epilogue

Ruby clutched her teacup perhaps a little too firmly as her eyes scanned the rest of A New Leaf. She'd come here early, partially because she could use an extra cup of tea to calm her nerves before her meeting, and partially because if she waited too long, she might have decided not to show up at all.

But now, as the clock on the wall ticked closer to the meeting time, she began to have her doubts. Would he be a no-show?

This was stupid. *"I never should have let you talk me into it."*

Clifford didn't even raise his head from where he lay in his designated doggy bed. *"I'm fairly shocked it worked. You never listen to my sage advice."*

"I hope it pans out."

"You and me both." He shut his eyes.

Ruby's breath caught her chest at the sound of the bell above the door. She turned to look and, sure enough, with three minutes to spare, there stood the breathtaking outline of Zax Banderfield.

He waved to Harley Hardtimes before looking around and spotting Ruby. The gleam in his eyes made her swallow hard and berate herself for her involuntary school-girl reactions.

"This seat taken?" he said, placing his hand on the back of it.

"Yes, I'm waiting for a gentleman to join me. He's tall, a member of the High Council, though I'm not sure what he actually *does* for that."

Zax chuckled and took his seat across the table from her. "I was glad to receive your invitation. But just so we're clear, did you call me here on another business matter?"

"Not this time. Although I will say that enjoying a bit of my time is considered serious business by most people around town."

"I'll try not to squander it, then." He winked and she sipped her tea to disguise her pleasure.

Harley hurried over, grinning down at Ruby like a fool before taking Zax's order. Once he nodded and left to get Zax a cup of coffee and a meat pie, the werebear leaned back in his chair, sighing deeply. "You heard anything from Bloom?"

"I thought I made it clear this wasn't about business."

"You did. But I don't like to jump straight into pleasure."

"Making me wait?"

"That implies you'll say yes when it comes time."

"You don't know that. I'm very mysterious."

He chuckled. "That you are."

Harley slipped the coffee and pie in front of Zax and promptly disappeared. Well, it was certainly nice to know someone else had her back around town.

"Swamy found Cedric's letters to Opal a day before he attacked Virgil," she said. "Bloom says that's what initiated the attack. He'd been planning for *something* for a while, but that was what triggered it."

Zax poured a small bit of cream into his coffee, stirring it lazily. "Shouldn't he have known they were from Cedric? Weren't they signed?"

"They were signed," she said. "They were signed 'pining for you.' Not exactly sneaky. Of course, because of what Swamy had seen transpire between Virgil and Opal, he was already fixated on the wrong Pine. He filled in the blank incorrectly."

"And once he found that out, he went back for the letters to expose Opal and frame Cedric for his disappearance?"

"Yes. Opal had stashed them in a small jewelry box, thinking Swamy would never find them there. But she says she'd found the box opened a couple of days before she noticed him missing. She wasn't sure if he'd read them, but she moved them all, just in case. They were tucked behind the headboard when he found them."

Zax grunted like the wind had been knocked from him. "That's cold. Hiding letters from your lover behind the headboard of the bed you share with your boyfriend?"

"I agree. Not the most honorable decision. But neither is cheating."

"Fair enough. But either way, it looks like I'm going to have to lead a sleuth-wide heart-to-heart about integrity and loyalty sometime soon. At least the letters were never published."

"Yes," Ruby agreed. "That's one small victory. Not just for Cedric and Opal, but for the general population. From what Bloom described, the letters aren't what anyone would call 'family friendly'."

"And I assume the sheriff had something to do with keeping them from being published?"

"She did. While she can't outright forbid the *Watch* from publishing whatever it wants, all she had to do was suggest to Arthur Flufferbum that publishing materials supplied by a man who had attacked two people and was going after a third when he was caught might not reflect well on the reputation of the *Eastwind Watch* and their policy of anonymous sources."

"That'll do it," Zax said.

Ruby paused before she spoke again. She was already pretty sure of the answer, but she needed to have it confirmed. Men could get away with all kinds of things due to women's desire to fill in the blanks with favorable assumptions. "You're not married, I assume?"

Zax raised his eyebrows. "Is this still business, or are we transitioning into pleasure?"

"That depends greatly upon your answer."

He leaned forward and shook his head. "Not married," he said quietly, his deep voice rumbling through her. "Used to be, but she left a long time ago."

Ruby pledged to learn more about that, but not now. "Girlfriend?"

"Not in a while."

"Boyfriend?"

"Not in a longer while."

And now it was Ruby's eyebrows that shot up toward her hairline. "Oh, this *will* be fun."

"What will?"

"Getting to know you outside of business."

"Ah," he said, tilting his head back. "You mean by talking."

She nodded.

"Then it seems you and I have different preferred methods for getting to know someone who fascinates us."

"It seems so. But seeing as how I set up this date, I also get to set the rules."

"This time," he said.

She nodded slowly. "Sure. This time."

The End of Book 1

Turn the page for more Ruby True—>

ELVES' BELLS
A Ruby True Magical Mystery 2

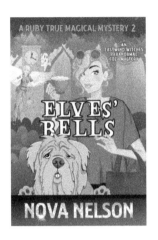

When an elf falls to his death from Eastwind's clock tower, a cryptic message on him points to Ruby True as the main suspect.

With the help of Sheriff Bloom's judgment and Clifford's nose, will they be able to sniff out the real culprit... before another Eastwinder dies?

Read Elves Bells now:
www.eastwindwitches.com/ruby2

Get an exclusive Eastwind Witches book - free!

The Missing Motive follows a murder that takes place two years before Nora arrives in Eastwind.

With Sheriff Bloom by her side, Ruby True attempts to figure out who killed the insufferable druid who has taken up residence in her home.

Enjoy the divine duo of True and Bloom, and visit some of your favorite Eastwind townsfolk in this humorous caper!

This book is only available to members of the Cozy Coven, Nova Nelson's reader group.

Click the link below to join and claim your book:

Join the Cozy Coven

Go to www.cozycoven.com

About the Author

Nova Nelson grew up on a steady diet of Agatha Christie novels. She loves the mind candy of cozy mysteries and has been weaving paranormal tales since she first learned handwriting. Those two loves meet in her Eastwind Witches series, and it's about time, if she does say so herself.

When she's not busy writing, she enjoys long walks with her strong-willed dogs and eating breakfast for dinner.

Say hello:
nova@novanelson.com

Printed in the USA
CPSIA information can be obtained
at www.ICGtesting.com
LVHW090131130424
777205LV00002B/347